Raphael
Forever

Rita Mitchell

PAPERBACK: 978-1-950256-96-9
EBOOK: 978-1-950256-97-6

Ordering Information:

For orders and inquiries, please contact:
1-888-375-9818
www.toplinkpublishing.com
bookorder@toplinkpublishing.com

Printed in the United States of America

This book is dedicated to a real Raphael,
James Raphael Willette who has been my
lifetime friend since childhood.

Love you, Rita

CHAPTER 1

October 14, 1951 was a gorgeous fall day. The sky was a heavenly blue and the crisp air reminded you it was fall, but a warm day for the middle of October. The maple trees lining both sides of the main street winding through the little town of Maple Valley, Kentucky were clinging to their red and yellow leaves, the bright sunshine giving them a fairytale glow.

Katie was getting ready to go to Skate World Skating Rink in downtown Louisville to meet up with a young soldier stationed at nearby Fort Knox. She had been meeting him there for a couple of months now. She would catch a public bus to the skating rink every weekend and back to Maple Valley after the rink closed. But tonight would be different because Joe now had his car on base and would drive her home.

"Katie", her little brother Ron, interrupted her thoughts, "Will you take me to my friend Raphael's house? He has a pony and said I could ride her if I would let him play with my helicopter."

His friend Raphael lived just across the street, but he had to cross a railroad track and the main street to get there. He was only seven years old and Mom did not like for him to go alone, but Katie knew he did it anyway if he couldn't find an escort.

Raphael's house was a bright white, with a small wrap-around corral hugging one end of the house. Inside the corral was a pretty black, brown, and white Indian pony with perfect markings of a white eagle on her rump and a less obvious brown and white buffalo on her left side. She is certainly a unique looking animal, Katie thought as she watched a little boy chasing her around the corral.

The pony was running in circles and shaking her head clearly stressed and unhappy about being chased. The boy was determined to get her over by the fence where a small white stool had been placed intended to assist him upon the pony's back, Katie assumed.

Ron had run ahead to help his friend calm the pony who was just as determined not to succumb to their plan. As Katie got closer, the boy stopped chasing the pony and stared at her, and Katie stared back in awe. "Hi," she said, "I'm Ron's big sister. You must be Raphael." He did not answer her, just kept staring.

Katie thought he was undoubtedly the most adorable male child she had ever seen. He had an abundance of thick brown hair that was quite unruly, and the most delicate, perfect skin, still brown from the summer sun. He was a bit taller than her brother and quite skinny, but it was the face that had her mesmerized. That little face was a perfect oval with a nose too big for the face. He had the longest, thickest lashes that framed his expressive huge brown eyes.

He was anxious to get on his pony and looked around as if he was expecting someone to be there to help. As he did not see who he was looking for, the elf- like child focused on Katie again. "Lady," he asked, "will you help me get on Nellie?"

As Katie was helping him upon the pony, she heard footsteps behind her. Must be who he was looking for, she thought. A tall blond girl appeared, apparently an older sister. The girl did not speak and neither did Katie.

Katie watched the boy ride away, waved at her brother and crossed the street on her way back home.

Somehow she knew that never in her lifetime would she forget that precious little boy, for his image would forever be etched in her memory.

Her thoughts quickly went back to Joe and the skating rink. She couldn't wait to see him again. He was her first serious boyfriend. She was not quite seventeen, and he was twenty, so he made her feel very grown up.

CHAPTER 2

The evening at the skating rink had been fun as always, but Katie was anxious to leave and ride in Joe's 48 Chevy he had told her about. It was a birthday gift last year from his parents, Mr. and Mrs. John and Marie Gibson. He had dodged the draft a couple of years working on his father's large cattle farm in Hopkinsville, Kentucky, but as the war accelerated, he had been drafted last April.

"I'm tired of skating," she told him as they were "skaing" around the rink for the tenth time. Do you want to go to Jerry's for a hamburger?" he asked. "That would be nice," she said, "but I want to get home early so you can meet my family."

When Katie saw Joe's car, she thought it was a pretty dark green and told him so. She was pleased when he came around to open the door for her. They were both nervous about Joe meeting her family for the first time. Her Dad was friendly as always and her Mom liked him but was concerned about him being 20, and she only 16. But her older sister, Alice was sixteen when she married Jeff. They had been married for three years and had a baby boy.

Katie and Joe's relationship grew and two more months had quickly gone by. They were almost inseparable. Christmas was only two weeks away and Katie had a birthday in February. She would be seventeen and was sure Joe would get her a ring for one of those occasions. But Christmas came and went with a pretty silk scarf from Joe. Her birthday was another disappointment, a dozen beautiful red roses, but no ring.

It was a warm June night, Katie and Joe went to the drive-in theater where they went often now that he had his car. After finishing their cokes and popcorn, Joe put his arm around her as he usually did.

"Katie", Joe said in a very nervous voice," you are so beautiful, baby, will you marry me next Saturday?" "I can't wait any longer to get you in my bed. I have big plans for you on our wedding night", he continued.

"Don't be silly, Joe," Katie said, "I won't be able to plan a wedding in a week, and I don't even have a ring yet." "You will just have to wait," she said with a sigh. "I want a beautiful wedding gown and flowers and bridesmaids.", she said dreaming. "And, Joe, it would be fun if you took me on a honeymoon," she smiled as she told him her dreams.

She had been looking through the bride magazines on the shelves at Carrithers Drug Store where she had worked after school since she was fourteen. She had dreamed of a wedding like the fabulous ones seen in those magazines.

Joe wondered how she planned to pay for it, he knew that her parents did not have money for an event like that. His parents could easily afford it, but would be so upset with him, marrying outside of his Catholic faith, he doubted they would even attend. He hoped Katie would settle for a small diamond and a ceremony at the Justice of Peace office. He would not marry her at all if she would consent to sex without the ceremony. But he couldn't help himself, he had to do what he had to do to get a piece of that girl. She was so innocent and looked like a child in the face. And he did love baby girls!

Katie would not budge from her dream and hoped Joe would buy her a ring soon. She was determined to have that dream wedding, no matter how long she had to save. "Joe," she pleaded, "Can't we have a September wedding?" "That is only 3 months away."

He agreed just to make her happy for the moment, knowing he would come up with something to make it happen long before then. He hugged her tight to him and once again told her how innocent and beautiful she looked and he loved her. "You look so much like your little sister, Lizzy. She is a beautiful little girl," he said, almost getting a hard on just thinking of the three year old.....

It was the fourth of July, neither Joe nor Katie had to work, so they went on their planned picnic at Deer Horn Lake. That was their favorite park and close to where Katie lived in Maple Valley. Katie enjoyed the beauty all around the Lake and loved feeding the many ducks who were always looking for a handout. After feeding the ducks, Katie and Joe walked over to the wooded area and spread their table cloth on the ground. Katie had made egg salad sandwiches with pickles and chips and of course brought along Joe's favorite, her Mother's famous deviled food cake. Joe stood up and leaned against the trunk of a big elm tree. "Come over here, Katie," he said. When she followed him over to the tree, he took a small black box from his pant pocket. Holding Katie's hand, he asked her "Will you marry me, Katie Baby?"

Although he had asked her a couple weeks ago at the drive-in theater, he wanted the mood to be just right and Katie couldn't refuse this time. "Yes, Yes," Katie blurted out, so happy to finally be getting a ring. He took the pearl ring with tiny diamonds around it from the box and placed it on Katie's finger. He was so happy that he had guessed her finger size and it fit perfectly. He then pulled her very close and kissed her. Katie felt his erection and was conscious of a fluttering feeling in the pit of her stomach.....

Katie had already asked her friend Lisa about sex. Lisa was nineteen and more knowledgeable on the subject than Katie who had only graduated a couple of months ago from high school. Lisa had been having sex with her boyfriend Curt for two years. Curt was also stationed at Fort "Know" like Joe. Lisa said they were getting married when Curt finished his four year tour of duty in the Army. Katie had thought about having sex with Joe, but decided to wait until they were married.

Lisa and Katie were having lunch at Harvey's Restaurant where everyone hung out to get the latest scoop on everyone in the neighborhood. Katie looked at Lisa and asked "What is sex like? I have read good things about it and have been told that it hurts, which is the truth?" Lisa's face lit up like the early sunrise, she smiled a big smile and answered, "Wonderful." "Curt is a good lover and never gets enough sex," she added and giggled.

"Gee, then it doesn't hurt?" the starry eyed Katie asked. "At first, it does." Lisa informed her, "but Curt was gentle the first time we did it and I loved it as much as he did after a couple of times." "You have to please your man in sex if you want to keep him," Lisa said and giggled again. The young Katie took it all seriously and hope that she could please her Joe. She was ready, she knew, but wanted that dream wedding first.

CHAPTER 3

O ne afternoon, a couple weeks after Joe had given her a ring, he came by the store to pick her up from work. She opened the car door and looked at Joe and smiled. "You have a really serious look on that handsome face, is something wrong?" she quickly added.

"Katie Baby" he always called her Baby, "I have some bad news. My unit is shipping to Korea in October, so we have to get married right away." "We can't" she said and felt tears coming to her eyes. "I don't have very much money saved for my wedding yet. "You will have to do with what you have," he said, with no apparent regret in his voice.

Katie loved Joe and wanted to make him happy and wanted to get married before he left for Korea. She promised him that she would see Lisa tomorrow and get her to help plan a cheaper wedding than the one she had in mind....

The next two weeks were busy for Katie and Lisa and even Joe. Lisa suggested that Katie have only two attendants, herself and Curt. "That will cut expenses and I will pay for my own dress and help you to get flowers for the church," Lisa said. Then you can use your money for your dress and accessories as that is what is the most important to you, "O.K. Katie", Lisa asked?

The next day they checked every bridal apparel shop in the city but could not find a gown that Katie liked and could afford.

"Doesn't your Mom sew?" Lisa asked. "Maybe your Mom could make your dress," Lisa encouraged Katie who was feeling pretty low at the moment. "Yes" Katie answered without much emotion, "she sews, but she may not feel like it since she is six months into her fifth pregnancy. She is also busy with 7 year old Ron and three year old Lizzy."

Her Mom did agree to make her dress, so the very next day Katie and Lisa went shopping at Baer's Fabric Shop and purchased white chantilly lace, white satin, and tiny white pearl buttons for the back of her gown. Next, they shopped for white satin heels for both girls and a pretty chiffon dress in a pale pink for Lisa.

Joe, in the meantime, had been busy for days finding a chapel and a minister that he could afford without asking his parents for money. He settled for a small chapel near the base that would accommodate the few guests that would be attending. Katie's Mom had already told them that she could not make the long car trip. His parents declined the invitation just as he had predicted. that left a couple of friends from the base, Katie's other friend Millie and her boyfriend, and maybe her sister Alice and her husband.

He was unable to find an available clergyman, but found a young Justice of the Peace who would perform the ceremony for only five dollars. Katie would never know he wasn't a minister, he schemed.

It was a hot afternoon, August 15, 1952. Lisa and Curt picked up Katie to drive her to the chapel. when they arrived, they saw a very short young man in a black suit talking to Joe outside in the yard. Katie assumed that he was a minister. Joe looked handsome in his black suit and pink shirt with a white tie. He had a white rose on his lapel, just as Katie had requested.

Curt joined the men who had now moved inside, while Katie and Lisa had disappeared into a small room behind the pulpit where they were to dress and then exit in a rear door and come into the front of the church.

Katie looked worried and Lisa asked, "What's wrong, Katie?" "I'm O.K." Katie answered her sadly, "this is certainly not the wedding I have dreamed of for months." "It is going to be alright," Lisa assured her, "you are going to be happy."

Lisa got into her dress and helped Katie into hers. She had brought her makeup bag with her to do her makeup and offered to do Katie's "No" Katie refused. Joe doesn't like me to wear makeup, says it makes me look too old." She did finally agree for Lisa to put on a bit of blush and lots of mascara on her long, already dark lashes.

Katie looked in the long mirror on one wall of the room. She was happy with her reflection. A small girl with an adorable figure, a round face, a soft flawless complexion, hazel green eyes like her favorite Aunt's and long, curly, almost auburn hair stared back at her.

Lisa also looked pretty in her pink dress with her white satin heels, and she had added a strand of pearls. Her makeup was superb as it always was and she had her long brown hair swept back and secured with a silver clip, her bangs barely touching her eyebrows.

Lisa did not walk down the aisle but joined Curt, Joe and the minister, already on the pulpit. Katie had gone around the church and was entering the front door. The time had come for Katie to walk down the short aisle by herself to meet Joe. Joe saw her and was pleased with how his tiny bride looked as she approached him. She is so beautiful and child-like he thought.

She wore a chantilly lace ballerina length dress with a scalloped hemline and scallops around the neck. the sleeves were long and pointed over the hand, and boasted a wide satin sash to match her shoes. Her shoulder length veil had a round crown of white satin roses. She carried a small white Bible with white rose buds and baby breath corsage sewn on it by her Mom. Her long thick hair was curled in long thin curls that swirled beneath her veil like shiny ribbons.

Suddenly she remembered the little boy Raphael and the way he had stared at her. She wondered if he would think she was pretty in her wedding dress. For a brisk moment, she felt sad that she had never seen him again. One day she vowed she would have a little boy who would look just like him.

She was standing facing Joe. The strange little minister had begun to stumble through a short speech, something about God joining man and woman together and no man could part them. She couldn't remember exactly what he said.

After finishing his short confusing speech, the little man looked at Joe. "Do you, Joe, take this woman, Katie, to be your lawfully wedded wife, to have and to hold til death do you part?" he said nervously. "I do" Joe responded. He then turned to Katie, "Do you, Katie, take this man Joe, to be your lawfully wedded husband to love and obey til death do you part? "I do," Katie almost whispered.

Since Joe had not bought them wedding rings, the weird minister pronounced them husband and wife. "You may kiss the bride," he said to Joe and looked at Katie with lifted eyebrows and a flirty smile that made Katie uncomfortable. She did not feel happy as she thought she should have. Something was wrong with the ceremony. She felt cheated, nothing, absolutely nothing had been as she dreamed it would be.

The proper witnesses signed the marriage certificate, and they turned to exit the chapel. When they walked outside there was no rice being thrown at them or loud well-wishers. She turned to Joe who was now holding her hand and walking toward the car. "Joe," Katie asked. "Can we go somewhere nice to eat, I want to show off my wedding dress?" There wasn't hardly anyone at the Chapel who hadn't already seen it.

"No, Baby" Joe answered while opening the car door for her. "We are taking some food to the cottage and there is a bottle of champagne waiting for us there too."

They proceeded to drive the three miles to the cottage in silence.

CHAPTER 4

When they arrived at the cottage, Joe opened her car door and picked her up to carry her inside. "You certainly look beautiful, my little bride," Joe said as he put her down inside the door.

Katie was in a better mood and began to explore her new home, while Joe went back to the car to get the food he had bought earlier. He had gotten food that he knew would not spoil in the car during the ceremony consisting of canned tuna, noodle soup, bread, and big dill pickles that he knew Katie loved.

His friend, Earl, had taken a bottle of champagne to the cottage yesterday to get it chilled. He told Joe that it was a wedding gift to him and his lovely wife.

While exploring, Katie first noticed the ceiling fan in the living room that was so huge it seemed to overpower the whole room. The walls were white and a big round green and white rug was in the middle of the room directly under the fan. A brown couch and chair took up most of the space with a matching table beside the chair. A white lamp with a bold green paper shade was on the table.

The kitchen was small with an unmatched stove and refrigerator side by side on one wall. A small wooden table and two chairs took up the rest of the space.

A large bedroom was across the hall from the kitchen with an adjoining bathroom that could not be reached without going through the bedroom. The bed was large and looked comfortable. It had a pretty blue bedspread and a matching curtain was hung on the one window near the bed.

Joe had come back into the cottage and was calling to her from the kitchen. He looked up at her as she entered the kitchen. "I will fix us some soup and sandwiches if you would like to change out of your wedding dress so you don't ruin it." "Why not? I will never wear it again, and I never got to show it off," she mumbled.

Katie had bought a cute pair of pink, short PJ's for her wedding night. She thought she would go ahead and put them on as it was still hot in the cottage, even after Joe had turned on the big fan in the living room and also the smaller one in the bedroom. Katie wanted to take a bath, but she knew Joe would have the food ready before she had time to do that. So she quickly changed into the little pink pajamas and pulled her curls back in a ponytail secured with a rubber band she found in her purse.

After making sure her pajamas were properly buttoned and her hair just right, she went back into the kitchen. Joe was pouring soup into bowls he had found in one of the two cabinets attached to the wall. "You look cute, Baby, but you don't look like I want my wife to look," Joe said to her as he looked her over. "Do me a favor" he continued. Go back into the bedroom and take off your pajama bottoms, but leave your top on, and no panties please! Hurry back to eat."

That is a strange request, she thought. She was shy, but remembered the minister had said she was to obey Joe, so she did as she was told. When she returned, Joe shook his head and frowned. "No, Katie, go back and put on your pajama bottom" he said. Katie was worried that he would not like her nude.

Finally, she got to sit down and eat. They had a short conversation about the wedding, and she told him how strange she thought the little short minister was. The minute she finished her last bite, Joe told her to go get naked and lie down on the bedspread. "I will be there as soon as I put these dirty dishes in the sink," he said.

He came into the bedroom about 10 minutes later holding two glasses of champagne which they sipped slowly while Joe stared at her naked body. After they finished their champagne, Joe sat the glasses on the table beside the bed and disappeared into the bathroom. Katie could hear him going through the bathroom cabinet looking for something. His friend, Earl, had brought Joe's stuff to the cottage when he brought the champagne yesterday, and Joe did not know where he put everything.

Katie's heart was pounding when Joe walked into the bedroom naked. She was curled up on her side of the bed. She was nervous, but excited. She was finally going to see what sex was all about. "Turn over on your back," Joe said. "I want to see you." She did as she was told. "For God's sake," Joe said and frowned, "spread your legs more, Katie," Joe ordered.

Katie was really getting embarrassed, and she wondered why Joe was not big and hard like the pictures Lisa had shown her of couples having sex.

"That is a disgusting mess," Joe said, "but don't worry, we can fix it, Katie. I'll be right back and he went into the bathroom again. This time he came back with his electric razor. "Spread your legs more, Katie, he said. She, once again, did as was told, and he began to shave off all her pubic hair. "That's better," he told her. After he finished shaving her, she noticed his penis had grown twice its size and stood out in front of him just like the pictures.

He began kissing her and touching her between the legs. He then placed his razor on its side and laid it on her clitoris. It was vibrating and humming fiercely. Katie felt a sensation she had never experienced. "Oh, Joe", she moaned, "that feels so good." "You haven't felt anything yet," he said and turned off the razor and put it on the table by the champagne glasses.

Joe picked up one of the big pillows and instructed Katie to put it under her little behind. He was sweating but shaking like he was cold.

"Spread those legs, Baby, here comes Daddy," he said and quickly shoved the whole thing inside her. Katie screamed and

I have to have it once more and please scream like you did the first time, it was so exciting," he told her as he was pushing that horrible thing inside her again.

As he plunged into her sore body, she silently begged that it would soon be over. She began to cry and thought she was going to throw up. "Oh, Katie Baby, Baby," Joe moaned. He pumped her over and over again and it felt like hours to Katie. After the warm liquid that seemed to stop it all, he pulled it out and laid beside her panting like a hot dog.

"Joe," she managed to say, "Will you get me a glass of cold water, I'm going to be sick?" "Sick", he said, "your little body is so tight and exciting, how could you be sick? Your crying was even better than the first time. After all, you are just a baby, Katie," Joe said and she noticed he had a wild, weird look on his face. Katie shivered and ran to the bathroom to throw up.

Joe finally got up and went to the kitchen to get her a glass of water. When he returned, Katie had gone back to bed to lie down. He gave her the water and whispered, "I love you, Baby Girl." He rubbed her belly and thighs, but this time did not touch her intimate parts.

"Why don't you take a warm bath and get dressed, Katie," we will go get a big ice cream cone, that will make my little girl happy." he told her as if nothing had happened. She would have agreed to anything to get out of that bedroom with him.

The bath felt so good, she didn't want to get out, but she was afraid if she didn't dress quickly that he would change his mind and do that to her again.

She wondered if something was wrong with her and if she needed to go to a doctor. Lisa never described pain like that. but she remembered she did not have any pubic hair, and she knew she would be too embarrassed to tell another man what Joe had done to her.

She quickly dressed and redid her ponytail. She was ready to go, even if her bottom hurt so badly she could barely walk. She decided not to mention the pain or soreness to Joe again. He acted like it was normal, so she was sure it would get better. Maybe she would get to like it, too. She did like the vibrating razor.

Joe was already outside waiting for her. This time he didn't go around and open the door for her, so she opened the door and climbed in. She whimpered when she sat down on the seat. "Is my baby's little bottom sore?" he asked and Katie thought he was concerned. "It will be O.K." she told him.

They went to the ice cream store near Fort Knox. Katie got a double dip of strawberry and Joe got chocolate. It was a hot evening and they were sitting at the table outside, so the ice cream began to melt quickly. "Lick fast, Katie," Joe said, "or the whole thing is going to be in your lap."

Everything is going to be O.K., she thought. She must be making a big thing out of what must be normal.

CHAPTER 5

The days and nights went by without much change. Joe was at the base all day, and Katie spent a lot of her time reading most anything she could come up with. She missed her job at Carrithers and was lonely for her friend, Lisa, whom she used to see most every day.

This sex routine with Joe was about the same. She accepted it, but hated it more each time. She had long quit crying and sometimes held her breath if he would hurt her.

She loved checking the mailbox for letters from her sister and Lisa. She especially enjoyed the free magazines she sometimes got from companies trying to sell subscriptions. Most of the time, the box was empty.

Today she opened the box and inside she saw a large postcard. Her heart raced when she read about an upcoming Miss or Mrs. Fort Knox pageant scheduled for December 10. The winner would receive a $100.00 gift certificate from Williams Department Store in downtown Louisville and a one year modeling contract with the Whiz Fizz Bottling Company. The first runner up would receive a $50.00 gift certificate and a one time contract with Whiz Fizz to model for an outdoor billboard in the Louisville area. Second runner up would receive a $25.00 gift certificate from Williams.

Katie thought Williams was very expensive and that most customers were older, married, and upper class women. Katie would walk by the store and admire their windows and dream of being an older lady, married to a husband with money. She thought she would buy lots of pretty stylish clothes for herself and her kids.

The pageant would be so much fun and she would have almost a month to prepare for it, if Joe would only give her permission, but she knew Joe would never let her do that.

She was so exicted by the time he got home. She ran to him and hugged and kissed him like she did before they were married. "Joe", she started, "I got this pageant advertisement in the mail today. "Joe, I want to enter it so badly. I am here alone so much with nothing to do and I love preparing for things. but I would need a new swimsuit. I could dye my wedding dress pink and wear my white satin heels," she told him all in one breath it seemed.

He thought for a moment and surprised her when he agreed that it would be fun for her. "If I allow you to enter this pageant, you have to do something exciting for me tonight. "Yes, yes", she told him, not caring what she had to do if she could only enter the pageant.

After dinner and the dishes were done, Katie heard Joe calling her from the bedroom. Joe was sitting on the bed naked. "Come my Baby," he said softly. "Take off your clothes and come to Daddy."

She always did as she was told. He looked at her and frowned. "So sorry my Katie, but you have been a very bad girl, you never satisfy Daddy anymore. You never cry and scream for Daddy. Come lay across my lap," he said, "you need a really good spanking.

She laid across his lap as he ordered her to do. He preceded to put his leg over her legs to keep her secured on his lap and to keep her from wiggling away. "Oh, what a beautiful little bottom," he said, "what a shame that I have to make it all red."

He began spanking her, easy at first. She could feel that he was getting an erection. The more excited he became, the harder he would hit her. She tried to get up, but he had her locked between his legs and her arms pinned under her own weight. "Please, Joe," she began to cry. That made him even more excited. He continued hitting her until her bottom was getting numb. It hurt so bad, she knew he was bruising her.

Finally, he quit and threw her upon the bed. "Get on your knees, he ordered, we are going to screw doggie style." "No," she heard herself say. She was already hurting too badly. "No" he repeated loudly. "You will if you want to be in that pageant." "O.K." she said and got upon her knees as he had ordered. He plunged into her again. Now she was hurting inside and out. Finally, he released that warm soothing liquid inside her and he fell over on his back and was doing that horrible panting again.

"Now, let's see your bottom," he said and pulled her over to him. "Oh, you poor baby," he said and started kissing and gently rubbing her bottom. "You have to start making Daddy happy again, so I don't have to spank my baby's butt so hard."

The next morning Katie got up and went to the bathroom and took a mirror and looked at her bottom. No wonder it was sore, she saw long purple marks on both sides where his fingers would strike her. She took a long warm bath and it felt a little better.

She dried off with her big white towel, dressed in her slacks and long sleeve white sweater. She went into the kitchen for a bowl of cereal. She felt better and her mood lightened when she realized she had earned her right to be in the pageant. She could now start planning for it.

She was always a planner and enjoyed that part as well as the actual event.

She would look in the Post Exchange for a swimsuit, dye her wedding dress pink, leaving the white satin sash to match her heels. Gosh, she thought, he was in a good mood after the spanking last night, she might even talk Joe into letting her get her hair cut into one of those short cute pixie styles sweeping the country. She was tired of her long, curly hair, maybe even get her nails done.

When Joe arrived home, he found Katie had made him his favorite dinner, pork chops, mashed potatoes, green beans, and cornbread. "Oh, my baby is happy about something," he said and came over and kissed her like he used to.

They enjoyed their dinner and Joe went to watch the television he had gotten from his parents for their pagan wedding gift, as his Mom called their wedding. But his parents thought she was pretty and seemed to like her. Katie joined Joe in the living room. He motioned her to come sit by him.

"Now, tell me what Baby needs for the pageant," he said as he put his arm around her. "Well" she started speaking slowly at first. "I will need a new swimsuit." She was getting more excited, "I would also like to get my hair cut in a pixie cut and would love to get my nails done."

Joe was getting quiet, just staring at her. "If you don't want me to cut my hair, I won't," she told him. She was getting anxious, wondering what she would have to do to earn all that. "Don't forget I'm wearing my wedding dress and shoes," she said, still hoping he might let her cut her hair and have her nails done.

Joe cupped her face in his hands and studied her for a full minute. "I think you might look younger with a pixie," he said "more like a little girl. Yes, we will definitely do the haircut and get a new swimsuit," one we can afford," he added. "Of course, I don't think anyone really wins those things" he voiced his opinion to her. "The winner already knows she is winning and knows she really isn't getting all that stuff, but you need to do something you enjoy," he said. "You deserve it after that spanking. I really do feel bad about spanking you so hard," he apologized, "but I loved the way you cried. And I think you learned a good lesson that you should always please Daddy, right Katie," he asked. "Yes, Joe, yes" she answered him. She was willing to do most anything to get to be in that pageant.

Katie got her hair cut and Joe loved it. He told her that she was adorable and let her get her nails done a pretty soft pink the next week.

On Saturday, Joe took her to the Exchange to get her swimsuit. She wanted pink, but could not find one that fit. She settled for a pretty green suit with the legs cut high that made her legs look longer.

She had practiced her walk and turns hundreds of times and wrote a poem about the lifespan of butterflies to read for her talent competition.

When the day of the pageant arrived, Katie was so excited. The host was introducing the girls in their formal wear. He smiled at her and then announced, "Now, I present to you, the beautiful Katie Gibson from Maple Valley, Kentucky. She walked across the stage just as she had practiced. She stood in front of the host and listened to the question he was asking her. "Katie, what is the most negative thing about being married to a soldier?" Katie thought for a moment. "Never knowing when your husband might be sent to war and leaving you alone to make major decisions in your everyday life," she answered and smiled at the audience who consisted of the contestants families and what looked like every soldier at Fort Knox. Neither Lisa or any one in her family could come.

Next was the talent competition, followed by the swimsuit contest. Joe thought her poem she had written was beautiful and she looked sexy in her new swimsuit. The contestants disappeared behind the curtain to redress in their formals again and to wait for the host to announce the winners.

The host first complimented all the girls on their beauty and talent. He paused for a few seconds and said, "I am happy to announce the second runner-up is Miss Ginger Wilson from Columbus, Georgia." When Ginger stepped out of line and walked forward, the audience clapped and the soldiers were yelling and whistling.

The host began to speak again. "I now present the first runner-up, Mrs. Katie Gibson," again announcing her hometown of Maple Valley, Kentucky. Joe jumped up from his seat, yelling, "Yes, that's my Baby."

Katie was so happy, she didn't mind that she did not win. She was accepting her awards while everyone was standing and clapping and yelling just like they did when Ginger was presented her award.

A pretty blond girl from Chicago won and was crowned Mrs. Fort Knox. Katie thought she was the prettiest and was happy for her.

After the winners posed for pictures, Katie was given a card with a date for her to pose for her billboard.

She was thrilled about posing for a Whiz Fizz ad and happy thinking about spending her $50.00 at Williams. She couldn't wait to tell Lisa. Lisa had wanted to come see her, but she had to work.

Joe seemed happy too, he was laughing and never mentioned anything about thinking the pageant was rigged.

Katie was excited too until it suddenly hit her, what does he have in store for me tonight. But he was in a joyful mood at the present and she asked him, "Can we go see my family and Lisa soon?" "I was thinking the same thing," he said, "we haven't seen the kids for a while."

It was still early when Joe suggested that they had had a long day and wanted to rest. He undressed and got in bed. After Katie put her pageant stuff away, she went into the bathroom to undress and brush her teeth. She never slept in her pajamas, because Joe always wanted her to go to bed nude.

She opened the bathroom door and looked into the bedroom. Hanging on the chair was Joe's big leather belt. She almost got sick. "Oh, no God," she prayed, "don't let him kill me." She remembered when he spanked her, the more excited he got the more and harder he hit her.

Joe looked up at her, "Katie, my little pageant baby, are you sick again, you are as white as a ghost." "Let's go to bed and celebrate." She thought of that intimidating belt again. She also remembered that he wanted her to scream and cry, so while he was raping her, she tried to accommodate him with her crying, which wasn't too difficult thinking that belt was yet to come.

After he finished, he held her close. "You were wonderful, Katie," he said and asked "Did it hurt much?" "Oh, yes," Katie told him, "almost like the firstnight," she lied. He was apparently satisfied and he never touched the belt. Maybe he was saving that for another night when he wasn't as happy with her, she thought.

CHAPTER 6

It was a Saturday, a month after the pageant, Joe did not have to report on base, and they left early to go visit Katie's parents just as he had promised her. Katie was elated to spend the night with her family and visit with Lisa on Sunday before she went back home.

There was very little traffic that early in the morning and they arrived at her Mom's earlier than they had planned. Her Mom was bathing her new baby sister, Emily.

That was the first time Katie had seen her and was surprised to see that she had so much red hair.

And Lizzy was so happy to see her and to tell her she had turned four years old. Ron adored Katie and was always happy to see her. He looked like he had grown since Katie had seen him. "Do you still play with Raphael, Ron?" she asked. She was hoping that he would come over and play with Ron and she would get to see him.

"Yes" Ron answered, "but he has gone with his family for the weekend to visit his grandparents.

She wondered how much he had changed and smiled as she thought of those beautiful big brown eyes. Katie was surprised how disappointed she was that she would not see him.

Katie enjoyed seeing her Mom and Dad, she was always close to her Dad. They had a nice visit. Her Mom was happy about her coming in second in the pageant. Joe had told the story like she was now famous.

At dinner, it seemed like everyone talked at the same time. That's the normal for big families.

After dinner, Katie helped her Mom with the dishes and she told Katie that Liz had taken over her big bed after she got married, so she would have to share it with Liz and Joe tonight.

Katie went to bed happy to be between Joe and Lizzie. She knew Joe would not bother her with Liz in the bed with them.

When she awoke in the morning, Liz was in between her and Joe. Katie hurried to use the bathroom before anyone else got up. She was in a hurry to eat breakfast and go see Lisa. She couldn't wait to see her friend again, she hadn't seen her since the wedding.

Liz came into the bathroom with her and peed. She pointed at her bottom. "Joe rubbed my pee pee last night and squeezed my butt," Liz told her. "My pee pee is sore." "You must have dreamed that, Liz," Katie told her. "Don't tell Mom. She will be real mad," Katie told her. Katie did not want to believe that was true so she simply dismissed it from her thoughts.

Joe was ready to leave after breakfast as soon as Katie was finishing her goodbyes to her family.

Curt was visiting Lisa for the weekend. Joe and Curt would ride around while Katie and Lisa caught up on the latest.

So Joe dropped Katie off and picked up Curt. They were all so happy to see each other.

Both girls began talking immediately after hugging. Lisa had gotten an engagement ring from Curt and wanted to show it off to Katie, and Katie couldn't wait to tell Lisa all about the pageant.

"Is Joe shipping out to Korea soon?" Lisa asked. "I thought he was going last October." Katie looked surprised as she had forgotten about it and realized that Joe had never mentioned it again. She wondered why Joe had lied about going to Korea. "Oh, we don't know yet, it has been delayed," Katie answered and made a mental note to ask him.

"Hey," Lisa said smiling, how's the sex going?" I'll bet by now you love it even more than me, if that is possible. Katie didn't want to share those hellish nights with Lisa or anybody else. She knew something was wrong with Joe or her and did not want to discuss it with Lisa.

"It's wonderful," she lied again and changed the subject. She truly was excited about modeling for the billboard and told Lisa she would tell her the details when she found out more. "I hope you can come shopping with me at Williams," Katie added. She felt like a real old married lady talking about shopping at Williams.

Their visit went well and they enjoyed being together as always. Joe and Curt were back far too soon and it was time for Katie and Joe to make the trip home. Katie felt sad leaving Lisa and wished she could stay with her. She also dreaded going home with Joe, he was so different when he was with their friends.

They both hugged again and Katie wanted to cry. "I will try to come visit you soon," Lisa promised, "and I will definitely go shopping with you."

CHAPTER 7

When Katie and Joe arrived home, Katie thought of what Liz had told her about Joe. She must have dreamed it, Katie thought again, but a little voice in her head kept saying, ask him.

Joe had brought in their suitcase and Katie was unpacking it when Joe came into the bedroom. "Nice visit with your family and our friends, wasn't it Baby," he asked. "And that little sister of yours is absolutely gorgeous."

Katie stopped unpacking and looked into Joe's eyes. "She said you touched her pee pee and made it sore, what did you do to her, Joe?"

"What are you asking me, Katie?" Joe asked and started cracking his knuckles like he always did when he was nervous.

"Stop unpacking, Katie, you can do it tomorrow," he said, he sound irritated. "I am tired and want to go to bed and make love to you, NOW!"

"I am too tired, can we wait until tomorrow night, Joe?" Katie knew she was being too brave and would probably pay for it later. "Are you telling me no, Katie?" "Get undressed now, he ordered her with a lot of impatience in his tone of voice. "I just decided I want to do something new tonight" and he got a mysterious look on his face. What could he possibly do that was different, Katie was thinking, and she thought of that dreaded belt. "O.K." she said, not wanting to make him any angrier. She took off her slacks and panties in one move. After removing her blouse, she started taking off her bra. Joe stopped her, "just get in bed, I don't care about that thing."

She slowly climbed in bed, Joe was already on his knees. "You know I want you on your knees, so turn over," he snapped. "Get that baby butt up in the air as far as you can get it and hurry."

He began playing with her vagina like he had never done before, rubbing it and putting two fingers into her moving them around until he got them real wet. "O.K., Katie," he said, "it is about to happen." He pinned her arms under her and held her between his legs.

He rubbed his wet fingers on her anus. He then quickly forced his hard penis into her anus as far as he could get it. Katie screamed in pain, he must have split her open, she thought. "Stop, stop right now," she begged. But he somehow managed to hold her in position to sodomize her for another two minutes before she could wiggle away from him.

He slapped her bottom and yelled, "What are you doing, Katie? I wasn't finished! That is why it would be better with little girls," he blurted out before he thought what he was saying, "They can't get away, just scream and cry because they love Daddy."

Katie leaped from the bed, her rectum bleeding and hurting. "You are crazy sick, Joe, and you did do that to my little sister." She ran to the bathroom and locked the door.

She heard him getting out of bed and dressing. "Please come out, Katie," he begged her, "I won't hurt you." He sounded like a scared child, so she slowly opened the bathroom door. Joe was sitting in the chair with his face cupped in his hands crying.

"I am so sorry, Katie," he told her as he looked into her eyes. "I wanted it to be good for you, you were not satisfied anymore, you seldom cried for me." Katie didn't even try to explain to him that she didn't cry because she liked it, but because he was inflicting pain on her.

She managed to get to the kitchen, she could barely walk without pain and to sit down on that hard chair was a real accomplishment. Joe fixed them both hot chocolate and sat down across from her.

He started talking about Curt and Lisa's engagement. How could he act like everything was normal and they were just making light conversation, Katie was thinking.

Joe said he was going to go back to bed. She told him that she was not sleepy and she was going to read her new magazine she got in the mail. She knew he knew she was upset and would not insist on her going back to bed. She slept on the couch for the rest of the night.

She awakened the next morning to find Joe had left for the base without waking her. She quickly grabbed her purse from the bedroom to check to see if she had any money left. She was pleased to find a twenty dollar bill tucked away with a grocery list in a zipped pocket.

She hurriedly packed as much of her belongings into the one suitcase as she could cram in. The other one she had taken to her Mom's a couple of days ago was already half-packed. She removed Joe's clothes from it and threw them on the bed and finished packing it with her stuff.

It was painful with every step she made, but she was used to pain and did what she had to do.

She ran the bathtub almost full of hot water, the one thing she counted on to soothe her sore bottom. She wanted to soak for an hour as she always did, but she quickly bathed, dressed, combed through her short hair and put on her warm coat and gloves. She picked up her suitcases and left the house.

It was difficult for her to walk and carry the heavy bags to the bus stop. She waited for twenty minutes in the freezing cold for the Greyhound to arrive. Once she got to the station in Louisville, she had to transfer to a city bus to take her to Maple Valley.

Katie knew her marriage was over and regretted that she had not gotten pregnant and had a precious baby boy that would look like Raphael. "Oh my God" she almost said out loud, "I love that little boy." That was a disturbing thought, because she wondered if she was sick like Joe. but she knew she would never hurt him in any way, so it must be different she hoped.

The bus stop was about three blocks from her parents house. She was tired, freezing, and hungry as she had not taken time to eat breakfast. The suitcases were heavy and she could barely walk without pain, especially on the side of the road without sidewalks.

She opened the door and walked in without knocking. Her Mom was nursing Emily and looked up startled. After all, she had been there yesterday. "Why are you home, where is Joe, what happened?" her mother fired several questions at her in one breath.

Katie did not want to tell her Mom or anyone else, ever, what had happened to her or Lizzy. She prayed that Liz had not told her Mom last night.

So she lied as she did often the past months and told her Mom that when they got home, she had gotten a letter to Joe from the mailbox and opened it. It was from another woman telling him that she loved him and would marry him when he got rid of his wife. She knew Joe would not tell them the truth, because he feared her Dad would kill him or at least send him to prison, if he ever found out.

After the shock and the conversations were over and her parents knew Katie was not going back, her Mom told her to move into Liz's room with her.

Katie enjoyed her Mom's good dinner of homemade bean soup and fried pork and biscuit sandwiches. She went to sleep holding her sweet little sister in her arms. "I'm so sorry, Lizzy," she whispered.

CHAPTER 8

Joe came home Monday afternoon to an empty house. He soon learned Katie had left him. He smiled, picked up his coat and headed for his car.

He knew that she would have gone to her parents. He was confident that she would never tell them about the little incident with her sister, Liz. He also knew she was afraid of him and would come home with him if he ordered her to. He thought of the fun he would have giving her the spanking of her life that she deserved.

Katie was looking out the window and saw him pull into the driveway and ran out to meet him. She ran out without her coat. It was freezing cold outside, so she had to get inside the car. She hoped he would not leave with her in the car.

Her Mom was busy in the house and her Dad was not home. For that, she was thankful. She knew she would have to get Joe to leave before he got home or Joe would find out about the lie she had told her parents about their breakup.

Her Dad had explained to her last night that a lot of young men have affairs with other women, but would never leave their wives.

As soon as Katie got in the car, Joe started talking. "Hi, Katie, Lizzy was lying, you know," he said. "And, Baby, you are my wife," he said in his best authoritative voice, "and I insist you come home with me."

"No," Katie said firmly, "I want a divorce." "I will not give you a divorce," he told her. "Oh, yes you will," Katie snapped back, "I told my parents about what you did to LIz," she lied. "And if you are here when Dad gets home, he will either kill you or see that you go to prison." Joe looked at her for a moment. She looked serious, maybe she did tell them he thought and started cracking his knuckles.

"If that is what you want, Katie, we can talk to a lawyer on base." He was getting nervous that her Dad may be home any minute. "Now, go in and get your stuff, it is a long ride back home," he ordered.

Katie looked at him and thought, didn't he hear anything I said? "No" she boldly told him. "No, Joe, I am not going anywhere with you and I will get my own attorney." I met this attorney, Mr. Leibson, whose office was a block from Carrithers, when I worked there. She wanted to avoid ever getting into his car again.

"I will get the attorney to mail you a notice with the date and time of the meeting. I will tell him to give you ample time to get there from Fort Knox," she told him and opened the car door to get out. "By the way, you will have to pay him," she ended the conversation and ran to the house.

Bitch, Joe thought, but agreed with her by nodding his head yes. He knew she had control at this point and had already started the car, anxious to get away before her Dad got home.

The appointment was set for two weeks from Friday. Mr. Leibson had mailed the information to Joe just as Katie had said he would.

Katie had painfully told her attorney the sordid story of her marriage except for the incident with Joe and Lizzy.

She didn't know why she kept defending Joe in that unforgivable attack on her baby sister, but she felt she had a part in it by not believing her in the first place. She simply wanted to forget it as soon as possible. She felt ashamed to be married to such a monster.

Mr. Leibson allowed her to file on grounds of spousal abuse and infidelity. Joe agreed on everything hoping by giving her anything she wanted that she would not tell anyone else about his lifestyle.

She had agreed to take nothing from Joe, including alimony. He really did not have any possessions other than his automobile anyway. She only wanted a normal life again.

"Not wanting alimony is O.K., Katie," Mr. Leibson told her, "but it will be a few months before the divorce is final, so I want you to continue receiving your government spouse allotment until it is final. You will need money to help you to get a place of your own to live and a car to drive to work when you find a job."

After signing the forms, Katie thanked her attorney, Joe paid him, and they walked out together. Joe walked in the direction his car was parked. Katie walked in the opposite direction toward the drugstore where Lisa was waiting for her. Joe yelled at her, "Bye, Baby, you were one hell of a piece of ass." Katie never answered him. She did not even look back.

Lisa was happy to see that Katie had not been crying. She had never believed Katie's story about the letter Joe had received, but she felt it was Katie's business, so she never confronted her about it. It was her job as her friend to support her and help her to get her life back again.

Katie stayed with her parents for two weeks, but it was not the same as before she was married, and the house was too small for one more person. Baby Emily would soon be sharing Liz's room where Katie was now staying.

Lisa was now working the early morning shift at Bell South as an operator. Curt only came to see her on weekends, so she was happy to help Katie find an apartment she could afford.

Lisa's Dad had a 41 Chevy that he no longer drove, but didn't want to sell it.

He offered to lend it to Katie until she could afford to buy a car.

Katie and Lisa had looked all day again for the right apartment for Katie. they were marking them off the ad section of the newspaper as they looked. "One more today", Lisa said. "O.K." agreed Katie.

It was an adorable large apartment on the third floor of an old Colonial house located in a good neighborhood by a city park. It was completely furnished with attractive furniture and was well within her allotment budget. She hoped she would find a job soon and could keep the apartment after her divorce.

Katie and Lisa were at Carrithers enjoying a chocolate malt at the soda fountain when Mr. Leibson walked in. He spotted the girls and walked over to them. "Hi, Katie, I was going to call you tonight. Might have you a job if you want it," he said. "I know the manager at the Flamingo Bar and Grill downtown near the courthouse. She is looking for a waitress to replace a girl who is leaving next week. She said the tips were extremely good because of the location. Her clientele are mostly judges, attorneys, and other courthouse employees."

"Oh, yes" Katie said excitingly, "I will go and see her, when?" "Tomorrow would be good," he said. I will call her and tell her you are coming."

Katie remembered that her appointment to model for the billboard was tomorrow and didn't know how long she would be there. "I have plans tomorrow. How about the day after tomorrow?" Katie asked. "That will be O.K.," he said and patted her on the head. "I think you are a brave young lady, and I want to help you all I can." She told him about her apartment and Lisa's Dad helping her out with his car. Mr. Leibson was happy for her. "I am sure you are going to be O.K. and will continue to grow up to be the Katie I will always be happy to have helped," he said and waved goodbye as he walked out the door. "I am a very lucky girl to have friends that are so willing to help me," Katie told Lisa as they continued enjoying their chocolate malts.

CHAPTER 9

Katie walked into the office of Kirkland Photo Studio. She told the receptionist who she was and handed her the card that had been given to her at the pageant. "Have a seat, Mrs. Gibson", the pretty girl smiled and motioned for her to sit in one of the plush chairs against the wall. The receptionist picked up the phone and told someone she was there.

Soon another lady came into the office and asked if she was Katie. "Yes", Katie said. "I'm Marie", the lady said, we are all set up for you."

Katie was taken to a room, or more like a booth, filled with buckets and bottles of liquids. The only other object in the room was a round table with what looked like a paint sprayer. "If you will take off all your clothes and hang them behind the curtain", Marie was saying, "I am going to give you a nice California tan."

Katie just stared at her. She remembered the last time she was told to do that. "It's okay", Marie said, "won't take but a few minutes and you will go into the dryer room", and she pointed to a door that Katie had thought was a closet. "Okay, Katie said and reluctantly did as she was told.

After the painting process, she stepped into the dryer room which was a closet with fans on three walls and one overhead. That process took about ten minutes. Marie gave her a robe and told her to follow her to the beauty salon. There, her hair was styled in a cute, wind-blown style, her nails done in a bright pink and very heavy makeup applied.

Her next stop was the wardrobe room where her clothes were hanging waiting for her to finish up and go home. But for now, she was given a small yellow and white striped bikini to put on. It barely covered her rear and she was a little embarrassed, but it was still fun.

The last room was surrounded by lights and tables filled with sand, stone, and leaves. A gentleman in the room smiled and shook hands with her, introducing himself as Jeff, the photographer who was going to take her picture for the billboard.

"Just relax and have a good time", he told her. He pushed one of the tables filled with sand over in front of a backdrop scene of the ocean, with a beautiful blue sky and a couple of fluffy white clouds. "Climb on the table, Katie, and lie down on your stomach," he instructed her. "Now, put your chin in your hands and give me a big smile. Good.", he said and took a Fizz Whiz bottle with a bright yellow straw and an oversized pair of sunglasses and positioned them in front of her in the sand. Jeff pushed her rear up in the air.

"Hold that position with your cute butt up in the air more", he instructed. He must have seen the fear in her face. "I will be touching you now, Katie, to pose you for the picture, okay?" he asked.

After the pose was satisfying to him, he told her to be very still and smile, smile, smile. the extremely bright lights went on all around her. It was like looking directly into the sun. Katie's eyes automatically closed.

"You have to keep your eyes wide open", Jeff said. "Your eyes will become accustomed in a few seconds."

"Just perfect", he said, after shooting a couple dozen pictures. "You can go back to wardrobe now. Someone will instruct you in removing the paint and you can dress and go home", Jeff said, and left her alone in the room. She hoped she could find her way to the right room.

She was given a bar of brown soap that looked like it had sand in it and a bottle of lotion. Marie told her to shower with the soap and then lotion her whole body.

"When you get dressed", Marie said, "stop and see the receptionist on your way out."

"Hey, was that fun?" the pretty girl asked. "I did one once", she told Katie. "It hung in Nashville for a year." She handed Katie a card with a date she could come back in to receive a copy of the finished picture Jeff would use for the billboard. "By the way, the picture will not go up until summer." Katie was excited.

The following day she went to The Flamingo Bar to see Annie about the job. She went in straight to the bar where a lady with long black hair pulled back in a ponytail was arranging bottles of liquor on a shelf. Katie asked where she could find Annie. "I'm Annie", the lady said. "I am the bar manager. What can I do for you?"

Katie introduced herself and told Annie that Mr. Leibson had sent her in to ask about the job opening up soon as a waitress.

"Yes", he told me you would be coming in today, but you look so young. How old are you?" Annie asked. "I am 18", Katie replied.

"You know that you can serve alcohol at 18, Katie, but you cannot accept drinks from the customers until you are 21", Annie said.

"Oh, that's okay, Annie. I don't drink anything with alcohol anyways", Katie answered.

Annie showed her around the bar, introduced her to Larry the bartender, Ott, the short order cook, and Patsy, the waitress. Patsy then took over and showed Katie the bar menu, how to greet customers and write orders. Katie thought she would never learn the names of all those drinks.

Annie came back and took her to the office to fill out the necessary forms. "Katie", Annie said, "you will have to buy your uniforms, short black skirts, white long-sleeved shirts, and a black bow tie with black stockings and black heels. Do you have the money today?" Annie asked.

"Yes", Katie told her and was so thankful that Mr. Leibson had told her she would need money to start, so she had saved $50. "Will that be enough?" she asked.

"More than enough", Annie said, "but you will have to buy your black heels and stockings. I will have your two uniforms by tomorrow. We will see you tomorrow at 3:30 for training, but you cannot start working on your own until you are trained. You are a very good looking young lady, and I think the customers will love you", she said and walked her to the door. Patsy yelled, "Good bye!"

By 2:45 the next day, Katie reported to work wearing her black heels and stockings. Annie gave her the skirts and shirts that fit perfect, a size two, and showed her where she could change. She was happy she had bought her heels and stockings on the way home yesterday....

Katie couldn't wait to start work on her own. Patsy was a good trainer and Katie thought the job was much easier than she had imagined.

Today, she left home early, so that she would have time to stop at Kirklands and pick up her picture. The receptionist remembered her. "Hello Katie", she said and took out an eight by ten brown envelope from her desk and handed it to Katie. "Your billboard will go up on July 1st at Highland Drive and Scott Avenue," she said, then answered her ringing phone.

"Thank you", Katie answered and left with her envelope. She practically ran to her car, she was so anxious to open the envelope and see her picture. When she looked at the picture, she was disappointed. Her legs looked so long that it made her appear much taller than her petite five foot. Her breasts looked huge and hung out of the bikini top. Not at all like her small firm breasts. Only her face and butt looked like her. No one will recognize me on the billboard as they drive by she thought, and stuffed the picture back into the envelope. As she did, she felt something at the bottom. How surprised she was to find a check for $50. She had no idea she was going to get paid for modeling and what a generous amount. That certainly made her day, since she had spent a good chunk of her last allotment for uniforms and gasoline to start her new job.

By the time she arrived at work, she had decided not to share her picture and story with her co-workers. She was so accustomed to hiding parts of her life, it was neither tempting nor difficult. She simply chose to forget about the pageant. Lisa had taken her to Williams Department Store where she had spent her prize money on perfume and a new skirt and sweater, so she had no reason to think of it again until the billboard went up.

CHAPTER 10

July of 53 had come quickly, Katie had driven by the billboard once and forgot about it. She only wished she had never been in that stupid pageant.

Her divorce had been final about that time, and she no longer received her allotment from the government, but she was doing well at her job at The Flamingo. Annie was great to work for and Patsy was like a second Mom.

She had bought her a car and still loved her apartment.

Several men had asked her out, but she was happy with her life the way it was.

Men scared her.

Her parents had moved the year before to a larger house out in the country. She went there most weekends that she was off from work to visit with her siblings and parents. She loved taking the kids for rides to get ice cream or to shop for new clothes.

Katie thought of the first time she had gone to their new house. It was on her Dad's birthday. She was taking a gift to him.

When she arrived at the house, she saw the kids were outside running and playing a game. She got out of the car when a young boy about eight or nine years old ran smack into her and knocked her package from her hands. "Sorry," he said, and stopped to pick it up. He looked into her eyes as he handed it to her. "You are Ron's big sister," he told her.

"Hi", Katie answered, "I know you, too. You are Raphael." He stared at her as he had done that day she had helped him on his pony.

Katie felt like she wanted to run away from his stare, and then wanted to hug him all in one instant. What is the matter with you, she asked herself. What is there to fear, he is a mere child. He had grown in height, but had the same adorable face and those beautiful brown eyes that could see into your soul.

He ran off to play, and Katie regained her senses and went into the house.

After visiting with her Mom and Dad, she took Emily out to play with the other kids. They were playing hide and seek, and she hid her eyes and let them all go hide.

When time for her to leave, she gave them all a hug, even Raphael. As she was backing the car out of the drive, she noticed Raphael was standing in the yard staring at her car. Something about that little boy she couldn't understand. Once again, she thought how much she wanted a little boy just like him.

Her thoughts were soon back to the present, that had been a year ago. Lisa had broken her engagement to Curt and was spending some fun time with Katie before she left for Boston to start her new job with States Airlines.

Lisa was sitting at a table waiting for Katie to get off from work. They were enjoying just being single girls and having fun together like before Katie was married.

Katie was getting ready to leave, when a couple of men came in and sat at the table next to where Lisa was sitting. They were in suits and ties as most of the customers, so Katie assumed they were new attorneys that she didn't recognize.

One was a blond about six feet tall and a smile that could merit a toothpaste ad. His teeth were perfect.

"Hi, young lady," he said as Katie approached his table. "Good afternoon to you", Katie responded, "What can I get you?"

"I am Bob and this is my friend, Fred, we would like a couple of Martinis, and I would like a date with you", he smiled and showed those beautiful teeth.

The drinks are coming up and I don't date", she said nodding toward Lisa. "My friend and I are going to a movie when I get off from work." "Fred and myself are law students at the University of Louisville. We are harmless and would love to join you two at the movies," Bob said. "I will take my bar exam next year when I am 22," he kept talking. "No, thank you, as I said, I don't date," Katie once again told him. "Later," Bob replied and drank his drink.

Bob came in every afternoon by himself for a week after that just to talk to Katie. She enjoyed talking to him. She told him that she went out to her parents house most weekends to play with her younger siblings. "That is not a life for a gorgeous young lady." "Please go out with me just once," he begged. "I can meet you here and you won't even have to give me your address if you don't want to." Someone at the bar had already told him she was divorced and had her own apartment.

"Okay," she said, "just this once if you will meet me here." Am I crazy, she told herself. He is a man and will want sex.

They had decided on the following Monday evening when she was off from work.

She was actually excited. She had not dated since her divorce. She had lots of encouragement to do so from Lisa, Patsy, and even her older sister who was ridiculously happy with her husband, Jeff, and was expecting her second child.

Katie tried on everything in her closet before settling for a navy and green plaid skirt and navy cashmere sweater she had bought with her modeling money. It was a classic outfit and would never go out of style. She finished the outfit with navy hose, heels and coat.

Her hair had grown out from her pixie and was down to her shoulders again and was thick and curly.

When she arrived at the bar, she saw Bob getting out of a red Porche and was now walking toward her car.

"Hi, you look beautiful," he said, "I have never seen you in anything but your uniform." "Thanks", Katie replied.

He opened her car door and asked if she would like to go into the bar and have a Coke while he had a beer. "Sure", Katie answered.

Patsy, Annie, and Larry all clapped when they came through the door, "about time", Patsy yelled.

After finishing their drinks, Bob asked if it was agreeable with her to have dinner at The Steak Corral. "That would be great", Katie told him beaming. She had never been there but knew it was one of Louisville's finest restaurants.

They ordered prime rib with baked potatoes and salad, "the most popular entree on the menu", Bob said.

After dinner they sat at the table and talked over coffee for another hour. Katie talked about her family, especially the younger kids, but she never mentioned Raphael.

"After I graduate from law school next year, I will be moving back to my hometown of South Bend, Indiana and go into a partnership practice with a friend of Dad's, he told her.

"What are you doing with your future, Katie?" he asked. "You won't want to work at a bar for the rest of your life, honey. Bar waitresses age early", Bob declared impressively. "Or do you think some guy like me will come along, grab you up and carry you off to his cave to have a bunch of babies?"

They both laughed and, for some reason, Katie thought of Raphael. She thought of those beautiful, expressive eyes and suddenly was satisfied with her life just the way it was, waitress or not.

Bob told her about his friend, Paul, who was a Navy recruiter. "He is looking for a few attractive females to join the Navy Reserve. That could be a real good future for the right woman, Katie", Bob encouraged her. I will bring him into the bar to meet you if you promise not to fall for him in his good looking uniform", he teased. "Most women do."

They finished their coffee, and Bob drove her back to the bar. He walked her to her car and put his arms around her. He sensed that she was getting nervous.

"It's okay, Katie, you can get by with a good night kiss tonight", and he gently kissed her on the lips and winked at her.

"I want to go out with you next Monday, May I?" he asked. "We can see a movie after an early dinner." Katie agreed that would be fun and said "Yes".

The next evening, Katie was working, Bob came in with his friends, Fred and Paul. He was certainly handsome in that sharp looking uniform just as Bob had said.

After Bob introduced him, Paul told Katie that he was looking for females to join the Navy Reserve. "You would get paid to spend a couple of weekends a month working in the offices at the Naval Ordinance Plant after going to basic training for a couple of weeks in Bainbridge, Maryland." "It could lead to a fine career, if you decided to go on active duty," he explained.

He then proceeded to ask her out, but she refused as Bob pretended to sock him in the face.

It sounded like fun and she told him she would think about it. He gave her a folder with some information before he left. Katie did find it interesting but wasn't ready to change her life in any way at this time. She thought, maybe someday.

CHAPTER 11

Katie had not seen her parents or siblings for a couple of months. Most of her off days were now spent with Bob. She had never invited him to go with her to meet her parents nor to ever go into her apartment. Bob was content to pick her up in front of her apartment building. He wanted as little personal involvement as possible. He knew he would never marry a cocktail waitress, but he wanted to enjoy her charms and beauty without attachments. He was planning on taking her to bed before he left Louisville next spring to return to his hometown of South Bend.

It was three weeks until Christmas, 1954. This was the third year she had played Santa for her siblings bringing them toys, shoes and warm coats. Her father had been laid off five years ago from a major railroad company and had never been successful in finding another good paying job. Her parents were so thankful for her help.

Bob had gone shopping with her to shop for her parents and the kids and thought it had been a lot of fun, but next weekend he had planned for them to be alone together without interruptions. He had bought Katie a gift and was going to give it to her after a candle light dinner at his apartment and an hour of love making.

School was out Christmas week and he was planning on going home to be with his parents and to talk with his father's friend, the attorney who had offered him a position as junior partner in his law firm after his graduation.

Katie had gone to work early and was sitting at the bar drinking a coke and talking to Ott when the door opened. She looked up and smiled. She motioned for him to come sit beside her. Bob came over, sat down on the stool, ordered a beer and winked at Katie.

"Is your shopping all finished?", he asked her.

"Yes", she replied, "I'm taking the gifts out next weekend, so I won't see you, okay?"

"No", Bob answered. "I am leaving for home Christmas week so I was hoping we could celebrate next weekend. I have some great plans for us, it is a secret and I will give you your gift then", he continued. He looked into her beautiful hazel eyes to see if she was excited. Katie's eyes always did a good job of speaking for her.

"Oh well", she said, "I guess I will go home Christmas weekend while you are away."

She left her thoughts wander to that weekend and the fun she would have with the kids. She was disappointed when she thought of Raphael not being there but she was sure he would be with his own family for that week. I will have to leave his Christmas present with Mom. She had debated for a month whether she would buy him a gift. She finally decided on a toy army truck and tank. It even had twelve little plastic soldiers with it. She had seen he and Ron playing soldiers one day when she was home. Ron still had his helicopter.

No one, not even Bob knew about Raphael. She could never explain to herself why she kept him a secret. Maybe because she could not explain her feelings for him. She didn't think of him as a younger brother, not as a little friend, and not even as her child, more like an image of the child she would someday have.

Two weeks went by quickly. She wrapped all her gifts and packed them in boxes ready to put in her car next weekend. She was excited about Christmas with the kids but she was also excited abou the big surprise Bob had for her tomorrow. She knew it was to be at Bob's apartment and wondered if it was a Christmas party with her and his friends.

He was going to pick her up at her apartment at 6:30. It was 6:15 and he was never late. She put on her long navy coat that she had worn on the first date with him last March. She had chosen her red knit dress that hugged her petite youthful breast and butt that he so admired. She added a gold bracelet that Lisa had given her last Christmas before she moved to Boston.

She locked the door of her apartment and walked down the two flights of stairs. As she walked out the first floor door, Bob was pulling up in his red Porsche. She opened the door and climbed in. Bob smiled and kissed her on the nose as he sometimes did.

Bob only lived about fifteen minutes from her place. Katie smiled as she wondered what a bachelors apartment would look like. They pulled into the drive of a beautiful old house and he parked his car inside a neat old carriage house that once housed an exquisite horse drawn carriage, she imagined. When they got out of the car, Katie followed him around to the front of the house.

"I live on the first floor and another law student lives on the second floor", he simply stated.

After going through a small foyer, they entered a huge room. Judging by the chandelier, it must have been a ballroom at one time, Katie assessed. The walls were all white and the hardwood floors well preserved. A long narrow white rug lay in front of a black leather couch. The only other rug was a white bear skin rug in front of a white brick fireplace.

Bob interrupted her inspection, "Give me your coat, Katie." After helping her out of her coat, Bob looked at her a minute taking in her whole body at one long glance. "Wow Katie, you look good enough to eat, maybe we won't need dinner", he said teasingly. He hurried to the bedroom to take Katie's coat and purse while Katie continued her visual tour of his living room. She was amazed at how immaculate it was.

A black leather chair was placed at one end of the couch with a small black table beside it. On the table was a tall, simple black lamp with a white shade and a framed picture of an attractive older couple. Katie assumed it was his parents.

The black coffee table in front of the couch held a round, wide green vase with calla lilies, and small wrapped Christmas gift.

At the other end of the room was a round table with two sea green velvet charis that matched the velvet cushions on the couch. Hanging over the couch was a large framed ocean painting with green and yellow seaweed and coral formations emerging right below the surface of the water. Only one more picture was on display of an ocean sunset hanging over the fireplace. Peaceful, Katie thought.

Her attention was drawn back to the table that was set for two with place mats the same sea green as the chairs. In the center of the table was a holly centerpiece that held two tall white candles. On the place mats were clear coral plates and matched linen napkins. Above the plates were clear wine glasses with a tiny coral stripe with gold stripes above and below the coral. She knew the silver was real. A gold ice bucket was on one side of the table holding a bottle of red wine.

"How beautiful", Katie told him, "I am impressed."

"Sure you have guessed I am making you dinner?" he grinned.

Katie followed Bob back to the kitchen that had been added off from the dining area, it too was all white. Two pots sat side by side on the stove. She knew by the smell that one pot held sauce that he must have made prior to today and the other held boiling water. She watched as Bob put a tablespoon of olive oil into the boiling water and broke up the spaghetti in the pot.

"Can I help?", Katie asked.

"You can get the salad and salad plates out of the fridge and put them on the table", he told her.

The clear salad bowl and plates matched the wine glasses with the thin coral and gold stripes. While the spaghetti was cooking, Bob opened the wine and poured both glasses about half full. He tasted his as he uttered, "real fine".

He placed spaghetti on the plates and drenched it with sauce. After putting a heaping amount of salad on the plates, he motioned

Katie to sit by pulling her chair out for her. Bob lit the candles and joined her at the table. Katie had never been so pleased with dinner.

The spaghetti sauce was as good as any professional cooks and the Caesar salad was superb. Katie had never had wine and was surprised how smooth and tasty it was.

While they ate, they talked briefly about his school, his future as an attorney, Katie's job which he seemed to disapprove and why she had decided not to join the Navy Reserve. But mostly they enjoyed the food and the beautiful ballads of Hugo Winterhalter Bob had put on the stereo when they first arrived.

After dinner, Katie helped clear the table and rinse the dishes and put them in the sink to be washed later. Bob led or pulled her to the couch. Katie felt warm, happy, giddy, and a little dizzy. She knew Bob had drank more than her and felt his too. Bob was holding her close to him while the music played on. He started to kiss her, soft sweet and gentle kisses at first. Suddenly he was more aggressive with his tongue searching hers. Katie had never been kissed like that before. She was enjoying it and soon joined in the passion.

While they were still kissing, Bob picked her up and carried her to his bedroom and threw her on his bed. He pulled her shoes off and threw them on the floor.

"What are you doing, Bob?", she asked when she managed to get her breath.

She was getting scared. Was he going to hurt her?

"What do you think, Katie?", he gasped between kisses. "You are divorced so I know you are not a virgin and you did damn well with those kisses. I know you are a good piece of ass, so relax and enjoy it", he said and reached under her dress that had slid thigh high when he threw her on the bed, and jerked her stockings and panties off in one swift jerk and threw them on the floor.

"I don't want to do this!", Katie shouted.

"Sure you do pretty Baby", he said and took the thing out of his pants and shoved it in her before she could get up in her intoxicated state of mind.

"Don't ever call me Baby and get off me, you are raping me!",
she screamed.

But it was too late, he was well into the act by then and would
not stop.

When he had finished and moved his heavy body off her,
she managed to get off the bed, grab her clothes and run to the
bathroom. She cleaned herself up with toilet paper and put her
hose and panties back on and straightened her dress. She got her
shoes from the bedroom.

When she returned to the living room, Bob had fastened his
pants, put his shirt tail back in and was putting more records on
the stereo. "Is he crazy", Katie thought, "does he think I am staying
here?"

"I'm sorry, Katie", I thought you wanted me to and I did not
want to leave tomorrow without making love to you, but I did not
plan it like this", he said. "Next time we will undress and I will
make real love to you. I have been crazy wanting you", he added.

"There won't be a next time!", Katie shouted. "Now get my coat
and take me home. I never want to see you again!", she shouted
even louder.

Bob knew what he had done and didn't know how to handle
it, so he just got her coat as she requested. He started to help her
into it but she grabbed it from him, put it on quickly and hurried
to the door.

"Please don't be mad at me", he pleaded when they got into
the car. "I am truly sorry Katie, please give me another chance,
please!", Bob begged.

But Katie never answered him. When they reached her
apartment building she practically jumped from the car and ran
to the door. She heard his car pull away as she was opening her
door. How much she appreciated her own humble apartment. I
will never go out with another man again she vowed. She wondered
if the gift on his coffee table was hers and what was in it. She was
happy that she had chosen not to get him a gift.

She returned to work the following Tuesday. Everyone could feel something was wrong with Katie. She was very quiet and not the friendly Katie they all knew.

"What happened, Katie, what's wrong?" Patsy asked. Bob and I broke up and I never want to talk about it again, Katie said, and gave them a cold, calculating stare.

Everyone went back to work. They knew Katie well enough to know the conversation was over.

Katie had filed one more phase of her life in her heart and mind under secret.

Katie never saw Bob again and as far as she knew, he had never been back into the bar. She assumed that once he graduated, he had gone back to Indiana.

The next weekend she spent with her family and enjoyed Christmas with the kids. She was disappointed that Raphael was not there, but she knew he would be with his family. She left him a Christmas present with her Mom as planned.

She did miss Bob and wondered if he ever missed her. Probably not, she thought, sex is the only reason men date. Katie wondered if she would ever get married and endure that pain again even to get her precious little Raphael she had so often dreamed about.

CHAPTER 12

It was Christmas Season 1955. Katie had spent Christmas with her family, that had become a normal routine. She was on her way home with her humble little gifts the kids had made for her. They were treasures to her.

When Katie arrived home she parked her car and got her mail from her box before going into the apartment. She was happy to have received a letter from Lisa. They tried to write occasionally to save money. Long distance calls were expensive for them, because they could never talk for only 5 minutes and hang up.

Lisa enjoyed her job as a stewardess for State Airline and was now engaged to a pilot from California.

Katie put her coat and packages down on the couch and hurriedly opened her letter.

Dear Katie,

I am going to be flying the breakfast hop this week, Boston to New York, early in the morning and back to Boston in the evening. It is boring and tiring but everyone assigned out of Boston has to share this duty. Some business people take this flight daily, mostly executives that live in Boston and work in New York.

Anyway, I am taking a three day pass and staying in New York for a couple of nights. Tom will be flying in also and will have a weekend lay over the same days.

We would like for you to join us in New York for those two nights. I want you to meet Tom, you will like him I know. By the way, do you have a new boyfriend yet? It has been about a year since you and Bob broke up, right?

I will send you a free first class pass and you can stay with me in my hotel room at the Waldorf. You shouldn't need much money. Your flight will leave Louisville Friday morning the 1st of February and arrive in New York at 1:10am. Your return flight to Louisville would leave at 10:00am Sunday.

If you don't have other plans, I hope you can come and celebrate your 21st birthday with us. That would be so much fun. Tom and I would have the celebration already planned and all you have to do is enjoy the day.

I would have called you, but I knew you had gone to your parents for Christmas and I wasn't sure what day you would be returning home or when you had to be back to work.

By the way, thank you for calling Mom on Christmas. She is lonely now with Dad gone. I know that she misses him so much and none of us kids go home often.

Hope this trip sounds like fun. I still miss my best friend. Let me know as soon as possible as I will only have a few days to finalize the plans.

Love, Lisa

Katie wanted to call Lisa right away. She was so excited about seeing Lisa and going to New York and flying as she had never been on a plane. It was eight o'clock in New York and Katie thought Lisa should be home. She picked up the phone and dialed long distance.

"Hello", Lisa answered the phone. "Hi", Katie answered. "I am so excited to spend my 21st birthday in New York with my best friend. That would be more than fantastic," she told her. "I have nothing planned," Katie admitted.

"I am also excited about flying", Katie told her. "I might decide that I would like to be a stewardess," she said laughing. Lisa sounded serious, "you can't be a stewardess, Katie, you are too short. You have to be 5 ft. 2 in. tall to reach the overhead storage bins." Katie thought Lisa's attitude sounded a bit superior since she was only kidding, but it didn't matter she probably wouldn't leave her siblings anyway.

They chatted for a few more minutes then said goodbye.

Being the planner that Katie was, she immediately started to make notes. Lisa had told her the New York winters were brutal. She made notes to purchase a warm coat, get a haircut, and go see the kids again before she left.

The days flew by and her trip was a couple days away. Annie was excited for her and told her to take off as many days as she needed for the trip. Of course, Patsy had to tell her to find a new man, which had gotten a response from Katie rolling her eyes.

Katie had gone to see the kids the previous weekend. They too were excited about her riding on a plane and asked many questions. Raphael was there and asked if she was afraid. "No", Katie told him, "it will be fun." He looked at her with those beautiful serious brown eyes. "Are you coming back?" he asked. "Of course, Raphael. I'm coming back, I wouldn't leave you," she answered and laughed.

Katie had gone shopping the day after the phone call and purchased a warm Mouton coat, a brown wool dress, and a lovely brown plaid scarf and gloves to go with it. She also bought a dark green cashmere sweater for Lisa. Lisa had done her hair blond, and Katie thought it would look pretty on her.

February 1st was here. Katie got up much earlier than she would have had to, but she was too excited to sleep. She checked her luggage one more time, got ready, and called a cab to take her to the airport.

The plane was loaded and taxiing down the runway for take-off. Katie had gotten a window seat and was watching the landscape race by when she felt the plane lifting off the ground.

About two hours in flight, the cute blond stewardess brought her lunch consisting of a turkey sandwich, potato salad, chips, a coke, and a chocolate chip cookie.

Soon, she arrived in New York. Lisa was there to meet her. "Hi," Lisa said and hugged her. "I love your Mouton and your hair is so cute!" Lisa said. "Thanks!" Katie said. "It was way too long. Bob liked my thick wild curls, so I wouldn't get it cut until now."

Lisa told a young man, apparently an airport worker, to get Katie's luggage and be sure to get it to the Waldorf Room 431 immediately and handed him the baggage claim. "Okay," Miss Lisa, he said, and laughingly bowed to her.

Lisa was right. It was bitter cold as they left the airport and hailed one of the waiting cabs.

Katie thought the Waldorf was the most beautiful place she had ever seen. Lisa interrupted her thoughts. "Won't do any sightseeing this trip, Katie, because you won't be here long enough and it is too darn cold!" Lisa said as she led her to the elevator.

Room 431 was nice and spacious with double beds and a pretty bathroom. Almost as soon as they got to the room, there was a knock at the door. Her luggage was there already. Lisa took the luggage and tipped the bellhop 50 cents.

Lisa and Katie had just finished unpacking Katie's suitcase when there was another knock on the door. Lisa went to open the door.

Two men were standing outside the door. One guy had black curly hair and skin that looked like he was never out of the sun even for a day. The other guy was a bit taller and had a body like a football player. His brown hair was cut very short, and he had long lashes that made him look like he wore mascara. Katie immediately thought of Raphael's huge, brown eyes and swallowed, more like a gulp.

Lisa and the man Katie guessed to be Tom were kissing. The other man walked over to Katie and said "I know you are Katie." "I am Kent." and lifted Katie's right hand and lightly kissed it. Katie retrieved her hand and looked at Lisa. "Sorry, this is my boyfriend, Tom, and Kent is his co-pilot and also your date while you are in New York," Lisa said. "You told me that you were not dating anyone, so I got you a date." "Why?" Katie asked. Lisa watched her face. The emotion was anger or fear. She didn't know which.

"Because young ladies don't go out in the evenings alone in New York," Lisa answered.

"Freshen up, Katie, and we will go out for an early dinner and get back early, so you can get a nice hot bath and get some rest before tomorrow. You must be tired after the trip." Lisa told her. "We have big plans for your birthday tomorrow!"

Katie started to get her coat. "You don't need a coat." Lisa said. "We will eat at the restaurant in the hotel. We can get a nice dinner at the restaurant on the 2nd floor or go to the coffee shop off from the lobby and have one of their famous burgers and fries. They chose the coffee shop.

While they were eating, Kent and Katie talked a lot, and Katie actually thought he might be a fun guy to go out with.

When they returned to the room, the guys ordered wine and a big bowl of chocolate-covered strawberries. Lisa and Tom sat on Lisa's bed, and Kent and Katie sat in the two charis.

About eight o'clock, Katie began to yawn. She was surprised that she was so tired.

Tom and Kent left to go to their rooms. Katie ran a tub of hot water and poured in some bubble bath. She soaked in the warm water for about 15 minutes, enjoying the smell of lavender all around her. After she dried off, she put on her pajamas and crawled in her bed. Lisa was on her bed still completely dressed reading a novel.

They started chatting, trying to catch up on each other's lives from the last time they had been together. Lisa asked Katie if she had dated anyone besides Bob since her divorce. Katie never answered. Lisa looked over at Katie who was sound asleep. Lisa went into the bathroom to shower and wash her hair.

The morning came and both girls woke up about the same time. Lisa looked over at Katie. "Happy Birthday, Katie! You can drink legally today!" she said. Lisa laughed and told Katie about her still talking to her after she had fallen asleep. They dressed and had breakfast brought to the room.

Lisa said she loved her green sweater Katie had brought her and would wear it that evening with her long black velvet skirt.

"It is way too cold to go sightseeing," Lisa repeated, "but if you would like to go to Bloomingdales, we can take a cab." "I think that would be fun!" Katie answered. "I brought some money I had saved. Maybe I will get a new dress for tonight."

"Bloomingdales was so large and so much to see, and it was also more expensive than Williams back home," Katie thought. "Let's go look in the bargain basement," Lisa suggested. "I have bought so many pretty things there that had been marked way down." "Oh, that would be great!" Katie answered.

Katie found a black silk dress that had a full skirt and white satin collar and cuffs that would be perfect with the black stockings and heels she had brought along.

Kent seemed to be a fun guy. Pretty eyes, but not handsome like Bob. Bob had that beautiful smile she remembered and wished it hadn't ended the way it did. She was sure she would have fun with Kent, however, as long as she didn't have to be alone with him.

At 5:00pm, the guys came to the room to pick up Lisa and Katie. "You look beautiful, Lady," Kent said to Katie. "You don't look so bad yourself," she told Kent. The guys both wore black suits, white shirts, and pretty ties.

Kent sensed that Katie was stressed about something...the unknown date with him he had guessed.

When he got her coat and was assisting her in it, he told her how pretty her coat was and started talking about how the fur was processed and made ready for apparel. Katie relaxed and they all left the room to get a cab.

They exited the cab in front of an overwhelmingly large restaurant called Mama Leona's.

The color Red seemed to engulf you as you entered the dining room...red carpet, red flocked wallpaper, and red velvet chairs. At one end was a large dance floor with musical instruments sitting along the wall and on the piano.

"This is the most popular restaurant in New York City and always has fine entertainment every night," Kent said. "Tonight Tommy Dorsey is playing."

Tom butted in and explained that the food was the best Italian food in the country and "I should know, being a wop myself!" he teased.

The hostess led them to a table beside the dance floor that Tom had reserved for them days ago. "Tom ordered dinner in advance. The menu is in Italian," Lisa explained. "Even with Tom's help, it would have taken us an hour to order."

Two bottles of red wine were in buckets on the table. The waiter opened the first bottle and poured a little in Tom's glass. He tasted it and nodded to the waiter, who then filled everyone's glasses.

"Happy Birthday, Katie!" they all said in unison and made a toast to her future happiness.

The dinner plates were brought to the table heaping with several Italian entrees, and Tom had asked for salad and Italian bread to be served with the meal.

The dinner was topped off with chocolate cake doused with a wine chocolate sauce and a candle on Katie's, of course.

Tommy Dorsey had been introduced to the house, and he stepped upon the platform and bowed.

The rest of the orchestra was introduced, and they began playing "Marie", one of his big hits.

After the fabulous dinner and the two bottles of wine were gone, Kent ordered the ladies Brandy Alexanders and he and Tom a bourbon and coke.

Katie was feeling her drinks, but felt safe with Lisa and was having a good time.

Kent asked Katie to dance and led her to the empty dance floor. The band was not playing. Mr. Dorsey was holding the mike and looked right at her. "Happy 21st Birthday, young lady. Let's wish this beautiful lady a wonderful time tonight and a great future," he said. Everyone clapped and the music began. Kent held her close and began to dance. It was a good feeling, and she was enjoying it.

Katie requested Mr. Dorsey to sing "I'll never smile again", and, of course, she and Kent danced. As the night moved on, Katie danced with Tom and Kent with Lisa. They all had a great time.

When the waiter came with the checks, he presented it to Tom, and, to Katie, he handed one of the exquisite menus. "This is for you to take back home with you," he said. Tommy Dorsey had signed it, "Best wishes to a lovely lady. Stay as sweet as you are, Tommy Dorsey". Katie knew she would keep that menu forever.

When they got back to the hotel, Katie thanked everyone for the amazing night. The guys went with them to their room, but did not come in. "We had better get to our rooms and get some sleep as we all fly tomorrow and Katie has the long flight home.

Tom kissed Lisa good night, and Kent gave Katie a hug. "Really was fun. I am a lucky guy to have gotten to celebrate the 21st birthday with a lovely Kentucky lady." "If I ever get to Louisville, I will give you a call," he said. "That would be nice," Katie said, and meant it.

She never again heard from him.

On the flight home, she was seated beside a tall black older man. The stewardess announced that a celebrity was aboard, Nat King Cole. Mr. Cole got up and bowed in each direction. He talked with Katie most of the way home. She found him to be a Godly, humble man. Before they reached Louisville, he handed her his signature with a best wishes message written on a piece of airline stationary.

What a birthday! she thought. This one will never be forgotten.

CHAPTER 13

Katie had been thinking about what Bob had said to her about not wanting to work at a bar all her life. She had worked at the Flamingo for over three years now and thought it might be time for her to move on. She knew she did not want to be like Patsy, working there when she was forty. She had no plans to ever get married again and wanted a career she could be proud of and support herself for a lifetime.

She had planned to go out to see the family, but at the last minute, called her Mom and told her she would not be out.

It was a beautiful warm May Monday, and she decided she wanted to go for a walk downtown. She would park her car on Third Street and walk past the interesting old houses, long ago turned into double or triple apartments. She passed by the house where Bob lived and wondered if he ever thought of her, and she wished, again, that their relationship had not ended the way it had.

She walked by the Whitner Community College. She stopped in front of the building and decided to go inside and check it out.

The receptionist referred her to a counselor that would help her with a curriculum that suited her needs and budget.

After taking a short test, she and Mrs. Green, the counselor, decided on a 2 year Associate Degree that would lead her to a hospital lab technician position after graduating and a two year internship training at the hospital.

Katie completed the paperwork to assure her tuition would be paid. The counselor said the new summer classes would begin on June 1st.

She was excited that she had made the first step toward her future career. She skipped the window shopping and went straight home.

Annie agreed with Katie that she had made a good decision and was happy that she would continue working evenings at the bar.

June the 1st, found Katie in her first class at Whitner as planned. Katie enjoyed the challenge and did well on her first assignment. She made herself a mental note to call Lisa that evening.

Friday, started out as an ordinary day. Katie went to class and later to her evening shift at the Flamingo.

When she arrived, Patsy was taking beer to a group of men Katie had not seen before. They were all dressed in jeans and dirty t-shirts and heavy work shoes except for the one wearing a clean neat blue shirt and khakis. All had hard hats lying at their feet. Must be construction workers working on the new bank building going up on 6th street, she thought They certainly are not from the courthouse where most of their customers came from.

The man in the blue shirt was very handsome. He had black curly hair and dark skin like Tom, Lisa's boyfriend who was Italian. When he smiled at Patsy, two very cute, deep dimples appeared.

Patsy motioned for Katie to come to the table. "This is Katie, gang. She will be taking care of you now cause Patsy is going home sweet home" she said and laughed.

"Okay, Miss Katie", one of the guys said "I'm Charlie". He then introduced all the other guys at the table. Katie forgot all the names except Ted, the guy in the blue with those darling dimples. She couldn't keep her eyes off him, and he noticed.

When the beer was finished and they were claiming their hard hats from under the table, Ted paid the tab and put a $2.00 tip in Katie's hand along with a business card.

Katie pulled the card from her pocket as soon as they were out the door. Ted Kaiser, Electrical Engineer, East End Electric

Company, with an address and telephone number printed on the card. What am I supposed to do with this she wondered.

The very next afternoon, a few minutes into her shift, Ted came in alone. Katie hurried over to the table to get his order. "A beer" Ted said, and "I want to talk to you." She took his beer to the table and he began, "Katie, I don't usually pick up waitresses at bars, just flirt with them." He looked directly into her eyes, "You are different, you have class, and I know you are a real lady. I want to get to know you better." "Will you come in early tomorrow and sit and talk with me?" he asked. "I'm not looking for a bed partner" he said. "I can get those anywhere. I want an intelligent young lady to share my time with. Your beautiful eyes captivate me, and you are certainly attractive."

Katie was surprised and before she realized what she was doing, she agreed to meet him tomorrow right after school. "What am I doing?" she thought after he left. "He is probably lying like a sailor."

She was so taken with him that she beat him to the bar the next day.

They sat and talked for two hours. She learned that he was from Bardstown, KY, was divorced, and had a young son who lived with his mother. Katie told him that she was divorced also, but did not elaborate. "I have no children of my own" she explained, "but I am very close to my three siblings and help my family in supporting them, because my Dad lost his job several years ago, and has not done very well since." "There is also this…" she stopped and never finished the sentence. Ted did not notice. She could not talk about Raphael, because she did not know who or what he was to her. She only knew she had this strange love for him.

"Do you bowl?" he suddenly asked. "I used to bowl on a league, but now my job takes me out of town a lot, so I had to give up the league and settle for fun bowling with my friends occasionally. "I have never bowled" Katie admitted, "but I would love to learn".

"I know I will be bowling on Sunday" he said. "Would you like to join me?". "I would indeed" she said. "I am sure it is lots of fun." "It would be fun teaching you" Ted replied.

"I will pick you up at four o'clock Sunday afternoon. Where do you live?" Ted asked.

"No", Katie said quickly. "Where do you bowl? I will meet you there."

"I bowl at Barstow Road Bowl" he answered, and they both agreed on those arrangements.

Katie found the bowling fun and Ted had commented that she was quite good for a beginner. She found Ted and his friends were friendly and gentleman. They all treated her like a lady with the respect she deserved.

"Katie, would you like to go to Bardstown with me next weekend?" Ted asked. "I want you to meet my parents and son." "I want you to know that my intentions are good and that you can trust me, Katie" he added. "Will you trust me and go with me?" he asked again.

"Yes, I think that would be fun." Katie answered without hesitation….and she did trust him.

She had asked Ted to pick her up in front of her apartment building. She watched for his new red pickup truck.

The ride to Barstow was a scenic one. Ted pulled into a driveway that led to a cute cape cod style house resting on the bank of a small lake or a large pond, Katie didn't know which. His parents were friendly and Ted Jr. was cute like his father with the same deep dimples. Katie was asked to stay for dinner. The dinner conversation gave her a lot of information about Ted. She learned that, after graduating from Texas A&M, where he received his Engineering Degree, he married a student from Fort Worth. She had gotten pregnant right away with Ted Jr. They had come to Bardstown to live. Ted had loved her a lot, but his job began to send him out of town for weeks at a time, and Nita hated the rural Bardstown atmosphere and being alone with Baby Ted. One day, she asked Mrs. Kaiser if she would take care of little Ted and let her visit her home in Fort Worth. She later called Ted and told him she wasn't coming back and wanted a divorce. She also said she would return for little Ted, but never did.

Katie had a pleasant visit at his home and invited Ted to meet her parents the following weekend. She surprised herself with that invitation. She had never even thought of inviting Bob to meet her family.

The next day she called her Mom and told her they were coming out the next weekend, the 4th of July. "I'll bring hotdogs, buns, and other stuff, Mom, if you will make potato salad and your famous chocolate cake", Katie asked. "I would love to and am happy to know you have a boyfriend." Mom answered. The kids started yelling and jumping up and down when their Mom told them Katie was coming for the holiday.

Her family loved him instantly. Her Mom thought he was very good looking. He brought Katie's Mom red roses and her Dad a neat pocket knife, white with an American flag on it. The kids got lots of red, white, and blue balloons that Katie and Ted helped blowup and tie with strings.

Everyone had a wonderful day and all looked forward to his next visit.

Raphael was not there, and Katie was relieved. She did not want to share him with Ted or anybody else.

Ted's company had sent him to Peru, Indiana for the next three weeks. Katie missed him, but she was busy at school and work, and she went to visit the kids one weekend. Raphael was there and ran up to her and hugged her like the other kids. She was so happy to see him. He and Ron were now close to 12 years old.

Ted called her every night about 10 minutes after she got home from work. On July 28th, Ted called at the usual time. "I am home, Katie, but I had to come to Bardstown for a couple of days, and I have something very important to do in Louisville before I come to see you." Ted said. He sounded excited and Katie wondered what surprise he had for her. She was a little worried as she remembered the last surprise Bob had for her. But Ted is different, she thought and dismissed that from her thoughts. Ted interrupted her thinking, "I will see you at noon Sunday." he said and hung up.

Ted was at her apartment at twelve Sunday morning as he had said. Katie now trusted him implicitly and allowed him to come into the apartment to pick her up for dates and, at times, to visit. He had kept his promise that he would not insist that she have sex with him.

Ted came in with a bottle of champagne and a big grin. He set the champagne on the table and went over and hugged Katie.

"Remember, I told you that I had something important to do before I saw you?" he asked. "Yes" Katie said, getting anxious. Ted poured them a glass of champagne. "I have a friend" he began, "who owns a Southern Auto store in Louisville on Miles Lane, and he is going to hire you as his bookkeeper. His wife is now doing the job but wants to quit work and have babies." Ted told Katie and laughed. "I will be happy to get you out of that bar", he said, "and we can be together every night, with Saturdays and Sundays free." Ted continued while he poured more champagne, "You can give your two week notice tomorrow night, Katie. Ray is expecting to meet you in the morning. I will go with you."

"But, Ted," Katie protested, "I go to school in the morning". "You will have to quit school." he said. I don't want you working in a hospital any way. You would be around all kinds of illnesses and work long hours and some nights again. This just makes more sense." he finished.

Katie thought, as she slowly sipped her champagne....Yes, she was really falling for this guy and had agreed that it was time for her to leave the Bar and maybe she didn't want to work at the hospital. "Okay, Ted, I will give my notice tomorrow after I meet with Ray." Katie said.

Mrs. Green was somewhat hostile and told her she needed to be more responsible. Katie dreaded to tell Annie after telling her that she would be there two more years while she was in school.

The guys wished her luck, Patsy cried, and Annie said she was happy for her, but had reservations about Ted's controlling actions without including Katie in the decisions for her future.

Katie had met with Ray and Jill on Monday morning. She liked both of them and they were impressed with her. Jill had shown her around and told her she would work with her as long as she felt she was needed. Katie was thrilled to know that she would have her own office and a salary of $80.00 weekly. That was almost double what she was making at the Flamingo. She was to begin her new job August 1st.

CHAPTER 14

Katie and Ted had been dating for nine months, and Ted had never asked her to go to bed with him. He thought it was time.

They had gone to a movie and out to dinner. Ted went up to her apartment with her. He put on a record, didn't even notice what it was. They sat down on the couch. Ted took Katie's hand and turned her face to him with his other hand. "Katie, I want to make love to you." Ted told her, "and, if we enjoy each other, then we will start thinking about marriage." "Is that okay with you?" he asked.

Katie panicked! "I don't want to get married again, and I don't like sex."

"You are shaking, Katie! What happened to you?" Ted asked. "You are warm and loving and would make a wonderful wife and mother." "No, No, No." Katie said.

"Let's talk about this honey. You are terrified!" Ted told her as he put his arm around her and held her close.

"Are you going to rape me, Ted?" Katie said, shaking in his arms. "Of course not, Katie! Is that what happened to you?" Ted asked gently.

Katie never told her sexual secrets to anybody, but felt she had to tell him to keep him from raping her. She told him about how she trusted Bob and went to his apartment and was raped. "Tell me about your husband, Katie. Did he hurt you?" Ted asked. "Yes, he did." Katie told him and began to cry. She said, "I have never told anyone that horrid story except my divorce attorney."

Ted held her and let her cry until she calmed down.

Finally, she got up and went to the bathroom and cleaned up her face that had makeup everywhere it didn't belong.

She went back into the living room and sat back down beside Ted. "I guess you won't want to go out with me anymore now." she said to him.

"Katie, of course, I want to go out with you, but it is time for you to get over all that." Ted told her.

"I promise, I will never hurt you. I have fallen in love with you, and it is normal for us to want to make love. Sex can be beautiful. It is a gift from God when enjoyed in love." he offered. "I will always do only what you want me to." he added.

When he left, he gave her a long kiss. "Tomorrow night, we will just touch each other, no intercourse," he said. He then looked at Katie and asked, "Do you trust me, Katie?" "I do." she replied.

The next evening, Ted brought pizza and cokes. We are not going out tonight, Katie," Ted said, and hugged her after he sat the pizza and cokes on the table. "Tonight is your first lesson in how to appreciate your body, Little One." Ted told her. The first thing I want you to know is that you only make love to someone you love," he said. "Do you love me, Katie?" he asked. "I think so," Katie answered him.

After they finished the pizza, Ted took her in his arms and asked her again, "Do you trust me, Katie?" "Yes, I do." she told him. Then let's go into your bedroom and enjoy each other..." Katie wanted to please him, for she had fallen for him completely. She also remembered Lisa telling her years ago that you had to please your man sexually, if you wanted to keep him.

"Now, let's both get undressed," he said, and touched her nose tenderly. "Don't forget, Katie. If I do something you don't like, tell me, and I will stop. Okay?" he said sincerely.

"Let me touch you first," Ted said. "Lie down and relax. Have you ever touched a penis?" he asked. After hearing the story of her marriage and the jerk she dated, he doubted it. "No." she answered nervously.

He began touching her face gently. He rubbed her forehead with his finger, moving around her hairline, touching her ears, and outlining her mouth. He moved down to her neck and farther to her breast. While massaging her one nipple with his thumb, he was softly caressing her other breast with the palm of his hand.

He stopped a brief moment and looked in her eyes. He saw no fear. He began rubbing her tummy moving slowly downward. He felt the soft hair around her vulva, feeling for the clitoris.

Katie quickly crossed her legs. "Please, Katie. I'm not going to hurt you." Ted said softly. She slowly uncrossed her legs and slightly opened them.

Ted found the tiny little bud and began rubbing it. Katie began to moan. He did not linger there as soon as he felt she was experiencing desire. "Turn over, Katie." She did as he asked, and he massaged her shoulders where he felt some stress. As he was rubbing her lower back and saw her cute rump practically in his face, he wondered how long he could continue this without devourering her.

"Enough for tonight, Katie. Did you enjoy me touching you?" he asked. Surprisingly, she did and answered, "Yes". "I liked you touching me, she said, but I still don't want to do it."

"That's okay," Ted said. "We won't, but I want you to touch me like I touched you." Katie gulped, but said "Okay". Ted laid down beside her. She touched his face poking her fingers in his dimples. They both laughed. She ran her fingers through his black curls on his head and down to the matching ones on his chest. She reached his tummy and began to sweat. "How can I touch that thing?" she thought, but took it in her hand and squeezed.

He had been able to keep in control until she touched his penis. It began to grow and Katie just looked at it. "Touch me again, Katie," he pleaded. She took it in her hand again, and Ted thought he was going to explode. "I'm turning over, Katie, rub my back." he said in defense of what he was thinking.

Ted could not take anymore. "Let's get dressed, Katie. We will continue tomorrow." "See, Katie," Ted said, "I did just what I told you I was going to do. Are you happy? Did you like touching?" "I think I did," she replied. Ted stayed for a couple more hours, and they finished up the cokes and watched television.

The next evening, Ted suggested they go out and eat a quick dinner before "Lesson 2" he called it.

When they returned to the apartment, Ted led her directly to her bedroom. "I'm not having intercourse with you tonight, so don't get stressed." Ted said. "I want to undress you. We may go a little further tonight, but if you don't like what I am doing, tell me to stop and I will."

He undressed her and got undressed himself. He laid down beside her and kissed her, a gentle kiss followed by hard, demanding kisses. "Find my tongue, Katie," he whispered. She remembered kissing Bob like that when she was intoxicated on the dinner wine.

"Are you sure you won't rape me tonight?" Katie raised up and looked him in the eyes. "Katie, I'm telling you for the last time…I will never rape you and will only do what you want me to." he said with a little annoyance in his voice.

He massaged her nipples again, and she couldn't believe how she enjoyed it. They became hard and turned a deep pink. He took one in his mouth and softly sucked. Ted moved his hand down to her soft little private mound and searched for the little button again. He found it and rubbed it quickly with his thumb and finger. She felt it pulsating as he pleasantly rubbed it back and forth. "Take my penis in your hand, Katie," he said, but never stopped massaging her clitoris. She did as he asked. He was hard and wet. She noticed she was getting wet, too. Suddenly, she felt like she had had a spasm. She jerked and stopped touching him. Ted knew she had had her first orgasm.

"Don't stop touching me," Ted said, as he flipped over on his back. He took Katie's hand and showed her how to pull the skin back and forth on his penis. "Faster, Katie, faster," he told her. "Don't stop." She was shocked when it spit a white liquid out on his stomach. She jumped from the bed. She remembered the warm fluid inside of her when Joe was raping her and how he would then quit the torture, but she had never seen it.

Ted reached down and got a towel from the floor and cleaned himself off. He held her in his arms and explained to her how that liquid or "sperm", was going to make them beautiful babies someday.

"Could she maybe really have her little Raphael after all," she wondered. "Tomorrow, we are going to do the real thing, Katie." "I think you are ready," he told her, looking into her eyes and trying to judge her readiness. Katie told him she was nervous about that, but she would try if he promised to stop if it hurt her. "I promised you already. Now stop worrying that pretty head." He pulled her over to him and kissed her.

The big night for Ted had arrived. "Everything should turn out okay," he thought. Katie now loved kissing and said the orgasm was exciting. He was so anxious when he arrived at her apartment, he didn't bother mentioning dinner…that would come later.

Katie was nervous, but willing to try. Ted led her to the bedroom. He slowly undressed her. He did not want to seem too anxious, but became hard just looking at her.

Ted reached for a condom from his wallet. "Here, Katie." He motioned to her to take the condom. "Put this on for me." Katie took it and tried to put in on his hard penis, but she was shaking so hard that he had to finish it himself.

He fondled her breast for a few minutes, touching her nipples until they hardened. He kissed her repeatedly and told her to touch his dressed penis and laughed. The condom felt strange to her.

Ted spread her legs and told her to relax. "Remember, I told you I will never hurt you." "I am going to put it in now, Katie. If you want me to pull it out, just tell me and I will immediately."

He placed his penis gently against her vagina. It felt warm, and he wanted to shove it into that prize package, but he slowly put a tiny bit at a time into the small opening. "You okay with it?" he asked her. "Yes," Katie said. "It feels good." He was soon all the way in and started moving it in and out. Katie held to him, but didn't move. He lifted her butt a little and increased the motion. Katie began to match his movements and moan.

"You are so wonderful, Katie," Ted told her after he had climaxed. "You too" she said proudly. Now, she finally had experienced the sex Lisa told her about.

They both got up at the same time and went to the bathroom to clean up. Ted took her to The Steak Corral for a steak dinner.

CHAPTER 15

June 10, 1959, Katie and Ted had been together for almost three years. Ted had long ago given up his rented mobile home and moved in with Katie. He had insisted on paying all the bills since she took care of the apartment and kept his clothes washed and ironed while she worked five days a week.

Ted had told her she needed to save money for a new car. Hers was running on its last leg. She had taken his advice and had saved a lot of money. He told her he would take her to get a new car this next weekend when he got home. He had been in Indianapolis for three weeks working but was coming home next week.

It was Saturday morning and Katie was restless. Too beautiful today to stay inside she told herself. She got dressed in white shorts and an pink tee shirt with butterflies on the front. She finished up with a thin white belt and strappy sandals.

She remembered seeing a pretty 57 Ford convertible on the car lot a couple of blocks from where she lived. I'll walk down to that lot and look at it, she planned as she looked out her window at the pretty flowers three stories below. She grabbed her little white leather purse she had taken to work yesterday and headed out to take her walk.

The car was still on the lot. A young man in a bright yellow shirt and a navy plaid tie sauntered over to her where she was admiring the convertible. He rolled his eyes in approval as he looked at her shapely body from her good looking legs to her pretty little breasts filling out that little pink tee shirt just right.

"Pretty car" he started, "I'm John and who is the pretty little lady?" "I'm Kate O'Bryan" she had taken her maiden name back and "I have been lusting for this car for two weeks," she responded. "Is your husband with you?" John asked as he looked her over from her head to her toes once more.

"No, I'm not married", she replied curtly, hating the insinuation that she needed a man to purchase a car. "I live a couple blocks from here and I work as a bookkeeper for the Southern Auto Store on Miles Lane. My boss is Ray Stivers", Katie volunteered.

"I know Ray", John answered, "we buy parts from him for our used cars." Since Katie had saved a large down payment, she knew she would not have a problem purchasing the car.

She drove off the car lot with the top down feeling like a movie star. John watched her drive off after he had tried to get a date with her and she had rejected him.

She filled the car with gas and headed for the country. She had nothing to do all day and knew the kids would enjoy a ride in her new car. Ron may not be there but the girls would love to go with her she knew.

Katie was driving along listening to the radio. Fats Domino was singing on "Blueberry Hill", one of her favorites of his. She was singing along and her thoughts turned to Raphael. She wondered if he ever thought about her. The boys were fifteen now and her Mom said they talked about girls a lot. She said they were seldom home anymore, probably at some little girls house she imagined.

She still dreamed of having her own baby Raphael someday. Sex with Ted was still good and they had stopped using birth control a year ago. Ted still talked about having a daughter but Katie never got pregnant and he never talked about marriage anymore. They both seemed to be happy with the way it was.

Her thoughts were interrupted by the site of her parents house. As she pulled into the driveway, she saw a small motorbike leaning against the house. The kickstand still in its upright position.

Her head felt as if it was going to explode, her face felt hot, and her hands sweaty. He's here she thought!

The kids came running out the door like school had just let out. They had heard the car pull in.

Ron ad Raphael beat the girls to the car. Raphael looked her straight in the eyes as he always did.

How cute he has gotten she thought but then he was always adorable. "Hi, Katie, long time, no see," he said. "Hi back" Katie answered.

Both Ron and Raphael jumped into the backseat without opening a door. "When did you get new wheels?" Ron asked, but before Katie could answer, Liz and Emily were squeezing into the front seat with her, both talking at the same time. "How about a ride, Kate?" Ron asked. She thought he sounded so grown up. He had never called her Kate before. "O.K.", Katie answered, "but not until I go in to see Mom and Dad." "Be patient, my little man", she teased Ron, and winked at Raphael who was still staring at her. "Leave the radio on", Ron requested.

They drove to Deer Horn Lake where Joe had proposed to her. She had never been back since that day. She temporarily felt sad and uncomfortable. She soon dismissed it from her mind and just enjoyed the kids.

The girls wanted to watch the ducks "Wish we had brought them food," Liz said. "Didn't think about it. I was being rushed," Katie answered.

The girls and Ron ran to the edge of the lake and Katie climbed upon a nearby picnic table. Raphael came over and set on the bench below her.

"How's life treating you, Katie?" Raphael asked when he sat down. "Heard you had a boyfriend, Ron really likes him." "He is a nice guy," Katie replied. "We have missed seeing you around," Raphael continued the conversation. "When we get back, I will take you for a ride on my wheels," he added proudly. "That will be fun," Katie said, and wondered how safe of a driver he was on that thing. She had never been on any kind of motorbike, small or large and was fearful of them, but she knew she would not tell him no.

After everyone hiked around the lake and had a good hour of fun they all loaded back in the car and went to the Dairy Queen for ice cream, Katie's treat.

As soon as they drove into the drive at home and the motor was turned off, Ron and Raphael jumped out just as they had got in.

"Time for me to take you for a ride," Raphael had not forgotten. She climbed on the back of the bike where Raphael had motioned her to sit. Katie was scared but never let Raphael know it. After about 10 minutes, she had settled down and was having fun. She noticed he was a relaxed and confident driver.

Located across the road from her parents house was a neighbor's pond where the kids went fishing. When they returned from their ride, Raphael rode through the open gate and into the field and stopped beside where Ron was fishing.

The field was rough and Katie thought she was falling off. She grabbed Raphael around the waist. Touching Raphael gave her feelings that she was not aware of. He is still a child, she convinced herself and settled with the excuse that she missed Ted.

"I will walk back to the house," she told Raphael. "Suit yourself," he answered, put the kickstand down this time and got off the bike.

Without warning, Raphael grabbed Katie's arm and was pulling her toward the pond. "Want to go for a swim?" he asked with a mischievous grin.

Ron jumped up from his crouched position on the pond bank leaving his fishing pole in the water. "I guess you know, Raphael, if you throw her in the pond that you will be in right behind her, you know there are snakes in that water.

Raphael let loose her arm so quickly she almost lost her balance. He quickly hopped back on his bike. "Forgot my fishing pole," he said. "And thanks, Katie, for the ride. Bye, be right back, Ron," he said as he sped away bouncing on the rough ground like a rubber ball. "Thanks for the bike ride," she muttered under her breath, unheard by anyone.

Katie turned to Ron, "I don't think he would have thrown me in the pond, Ron," thinking he had overdone the protection thing.

"Yes, he would have, Katie, he is as mean as hell," Ron told her. "Watch your language, young man," Katie chastised him.

She walked across the field and crossed the road to the house. After spending more time with her parents and sisters, she told them she would see them soon and went to her car thinking of the long trip back home. Ted would be calling her at his regular time and if she wasn't home, he would be upset.

She glanced over at the pond. Raphael had returned with his fishing pole and they were both fishing.

What are these feelings I'm having for Raphael, she wondered. I am so confused. Maybe I should avoid being near him. I will call Mom first before I go out to be sure he isn't there.

CHAPTER 16

Katie hurried home and as she was unlocking the door, her phone rang. She quickly ran and picked it up thinking it was Ted and she didn't want him to hang up. "Hi, Katie," he drawled in his sexiest voice. "What did you do all day?" "Did you miss me?"

"Of course," she answered the last question and knew she really must have.

Why else would she have had those strange feelings she had experienced riding with Raphael. Too absurd to think that she could be aroused by a fourteen year old. Although she knew she loved him, just couldn't put a label on what kind of love.

"You there, Katie?" Ted asked wondering why the silence. "Yes, I'm here Ted, I have had an exciting day."

"I bought that convertible I told you about and drove out to Mom's to pick up the kids." "We went to the lake and fooled around and to the Dairy Queen for ice cream."

"Ron was there and went with us. I hadn't seen him for awhile. Seems like he has grown two inches in height and gotten more broad shouldered. He even talks older."

She never mentioned seeing Raphael but then she never spoke of him to anybody except her Mom.

"I need to go out to see them when I get home," Ted interrupted her." "But first I have to go to Bardstown to see my son for a couple of days.

His voice changed to the authoritative voice he usually reserved for the guys who worked for him. "Katie, why did you go buy that car without me?" "I told you I would go with you to buy one when I came home."

"It is O.K.," Katie said ignoring the change in his voice, "I made sure that I got a good deal and all the warranties that were offered. The salesman knew Ray and I had an ample down payment to keep the payments low.

"Are you going to be picking up guys in that hot car, Katie?" Ted teased. "Only you," she answered.

"Ted, hurry up," a female voice said in the background. "Who was that?" Katie asked. "I'm on the bar phone and the waitress wants to use the phone," Ted clarified. "See you in a few days," he said and hung up.

Katie tried to dismiss it from her mind, but thinking of how smooth and handsome he is, she could see why any female would be attracted to him. She also remembered what he had told her when they first met, that he would flirt and sleep with waitresses but wouldn't marry one.

She wanted to talk to Lisa. The phone rang until Lisa's answering machine picked up. After listening to her message, Katie left one of her own. "Really want to talk to you, Lisa, but I guess you are away on an overnight trip or out having fun. Call me when you can. Miss you."

Katie took a shower and went to bed early. It had been a long day. She went to sleep immediately. She woke up about eleven sweaty and shaky. She had dreamed a strange dream about Raphael making love to her. I have to avoid seeing him, she vowed.

It was late and she had never called Ted when he was out of town, he always called her. she called the number he had given her for an emergency. When the hotel operator answered, she asked for Ted Kaiser's room. The phone rang and rang, he did not answer, after ten rings, the hotel operator said, "I don't think he is in at this time, Ma'am." She thanked her and hung up.

She didn't want to go back to sleep and chance dreaming of Raphael again.

She read for awhile and got up and made her bacon, eggs, and toast. After finishing her early breakfast, she decided to take a relaxing bubble bath and get ready early to go to church. She had not attended church for a long time and she thought it was about time.

After church, she went home to bake cookies and read some more. She was glad that she had bought several books her last trip to the bookstore.

After being up most of the night before, she went to sleep reading and slept sound for several hours. She woke up about seven a.m., got up and dressed, had coffee and went into work early.

When she pulled into the parking lot, Ray was also pulling in. He got out of his car and walked over to Katie's car. "Wow," he said, "a lot of car for such a little girl, very pretty, Katie." John had called him for a reference. "I told John when he called that if he didn't sell you that car, I was cutting out all his discounts." They both laughed and went into the store.

Around noon, she heard a familiar voice in the store talking to Ray. The voice suddenly popped his head into her office. It was Mark, Ted's cousin who looked more like a brother than a cousin. Same dark curly hair and olive skin, and good looking features minus the dimples.

"Hi, Katie," he said, "I'm going to dinner at Steak Corral this evening and thought you might be bored and want to ride along. Most females don't turn down a free dinner," he said and winked at her. "Yes, I would like that," Katie answered. Ted will be home in a few days after a short trip to Bardstown. I will be so happy. I miss him so much." Mark ignored her talking about Ted.

I know that Ted calls you around five everyday when you get home from work, so I will pick you up at six o'clock. "Will that work for you, Captain?" he asked and laid his hand on her shoulder. "That's O.K., Sir," she answered with a little salute.

That little gesture brought back memories of Bob's friend, Paul, she thought was his name, the Navy recruiter. She may go see him one day she was thinking. Ted is away so much, maybe that would be an interesting way for me to spend some spare time. She wrote Check on Navy Reserve at the top of her calendar and went back to work.

Katie was waiting for Ted's call, she was going to tell him she was going to dinner with Mark. She thought he would be happy to know she wasn't eating alone for a change. Ted never called.

She freshened up and changed into a pretty blue sheaf dress with a matching belt, added pearls and white sandals. She didn't feel like she was going out on Ted since Mark was family and sometimes hung out with them when Ted was home.

Mark came right at six and they left for The Steak Corral for an early dinner. Even without reservations, arriving early privileged them excellent seating.

Katie passed on the wine and went ahead and ordered her forever favorite, the prime rib with caeser salad and a melt in your mouth fluffy baked potato.

They talked about her new car, how well she liked her job at Southern Auto, about his job and finally it got around to her and Ted.

"I forgot to tell you how gorgeous you look tonight, Katie," Mark struggled through the statement and started fidgeting like he was about to say something that might be uncomfortable for him to say. Finally, he just blurted it out. "Ted is sleeping with a waitress up at the hotel where he is staying." "Ted told me that she was a cute little Mexican girl, but you are his real woman, his property, and for me to leave you alone." "You see, Katie, I've always wanted to date you. I could give you a much more normal life, maybe even a real marriage."

"Why are you saying this to me, Mark?" Katie asked. "Because I thought you needed to know what was going on and how I feel about you."

Katie finished her dinner as politely as she could, but her heart was no longer into it. How could she always judge men so incorrectly. She thought she was having a casual dinner with a future relative and now it has turned out to be a horror story just as most of her male relationships have been.

She feared she was going to have a fight with Mark when they arrived back at her apartment.

When leaving the restaurant, Mark asked if she would like to go to the Flamingo for a drink. "No, thank you, Mark, thanks for the lovely dinner, I have to get home early. I have chores that need to be done before bedtime," she replied.

They arrived at the apartment and Mark asked her if he should walk her to her door. "That's not necessary," Katie answered and opened her car door and ran to her apartment.

She closed the door and went directly to her bedroom. She started to cry and was wondering if maybe it was a lie and Mark was trying to break her and Ted up.

Her phone rang, maybe it's Lisa returning her call, she certainly hoped it wasn't Mark and Ted never called at this time. She picked up the phone.

"Hi, Katie. Out running around on me in that sexy car?" Ted's impatient voice came through the phone. I called you an hour ago, but you were not home.

After Katie caught her breath and gathered her thoughts, she sighed and answered "Hi to you silly, of course, I wasn't running around on you, in fact I went to dinner with your cousin, Mark. He came into the store today to make a purchase for his automobile and said he was going to The Steak Corral for dinner tonight and asked if I would like to ride along.

A long silence was Ted's immediate answer. She hoped he would not make a big thing of it and decided not to tell him about their conversation. She wanted to keep the whole incident as casual as she previously thought it to be.

"Katie," Ted sounded very serious. "Mark is bad news for us. He has always been jealous of me, even as a kid because I always got better grades in school, the best summer jobs and the cutest girls, even though he is almost the spitting image of me."

"He wants us to break up and thinks if we do that he we will have a chance with you. He says he knows he could make a sexy chick like you happier than I could." "Is that what you are now, Katie, a sexy chick?" Ted asked.

"Don't know where this is going, Ted" Katie answered nervously, but you know that I love you and miss you very much." "Certainly hope you will be in a better mood when you get home. I am truly sorry that I innocently went to dinner with Mark," she added.

"Me, too" Ted answered, "try to be home tomorrow when I call, Ted ordered and hung up the phone.

He must still love me and Mark is lying about him. She really was anxious to see him. She went to bed satisfied that all was well with them.

CHAPTER 17

But Ted didn't make it home that weekend. He had called to tell her there was a problem on the job and the deadline for completion had been moved up. He said he would be unable to leave since they were working seven days a week.

In fact, she had not seen him since before the dinner with Mark that he had never forgiven her for. He always brought it up in their conversations on the phone.

On the 5th of August, he walked through the door. He had not called to tell her he was coming home. Her first thoughts were how handsome he is.

Ted put his luggage down inside the door and grabbed her up in his arms. "Katie, my Katie," he moaned. I miss you so much when I am away from you."

It was almost dinner time and Katie quickly asked if he wanted to go out to eat or order pizza. She always wanted to feed him when he first got home from a long trip.

"I don't want food, you silly woman," he said and picked her up and carried her to the bedroom. He laid her gently on the bed and laid on top of her, started kissing her and undressing her at the same time. He kissed her forehead, her eyelids, her nose and, finally, her mouth. He wanted to taste her all over.

He pulled her shirt over her head not bothering to unbutton it. Next came the bra. He was fondling her breast with one hand while undressing himself with the other.

Next came her skirt, she had kicked off her sandals when he carried her into the bedroom. He kissed her belly button as he reached for her blue satin panties and slowly pulled them down to her toes and sneaked a look at the delightful sight underneath them.

Katie looked at his now nude, gorgeous body and touched his erection that was so hard it wouldn't bend in any direction.

Ted reached down to touch the warm, wet little opening that was waiting for him. He slowly pushed his manhood into it, and Katie yelled in pleasure.

"I love you so much, Ted, and miss the wonderful sex that you taught me to enjoy," Katie whispered. Ted did not answer her, not even the me too she was accustomed to hearing him say.

After they both reached their utopia stage, Ted lay on her exhausted, his heart beating madly.

Ted managed to get up off her and looked her in the eyes. "Bet Mark can't do that to you, can he Katie?" he asked. Katie looked hurt and answered him sadly. "Mark has never made love to me, Ted." "No," he replied, but I bet he loved screwing you."

Katie was shocked, angry and hurt. She couldn't even cry. She jumped up and dressed and without saying another word to him, picked up her purse and went out the door.

She drove straight to K.T.'s, a local bar where she knew Mark hung out, please be there, Mark, she silently asked him.

On entering the bar, she saw him sitting at the bar beside a plump, but attractive blond girl.

Katie ran up to him and pulled at his sleeve. "Mark, you have to come home with me," she said and finally began to cry. Mark held her to him. "Katie, control yourself, what happened, is Ted at home? Has something happened to him?" he asked all in one breath.

"Ted thinks we had sex," she answered through sobs, "you have to come home with me and clear this up, please!" she begged.

Mark was getting nervous. He couldn't go home with Katie. If Ted was that angry and he showed up with her, Ted would surely attack him before he could explain anything.

"There is a phone booth right outside the door, Katie, we will call him, he tried to tell her calmly, not wanting her to get more upset and demand that he go see Ted.

The phone rang and Ted grabbed it up quickly afraid she would hang up. "Where are you, Katie, please come home. I just go crazy if I think you have sex with anybody else," Ted pleaded. "I am so sorry, Katie."

"Wasting your breath cuz, this is Mark, Katie wants me to tell you that we have never had sex. What is the matter with you? I would never do that to you," he lied. But thinking of making love to that little sex pot made his blood boil. "Tell her to come home, Mark. I'm sorry," Ted apologized to Mark.

When Katie returned to the apartment, Ted was drinking a beer and looking out the window.

"I'm so sorry, Katie," he told her as he pulled her into his arms and planted little kisses on the top of her head.

Ted was so good to her the next few days making love to her every night and telling her how much he loved her.

Friday, Ted told her he needed to go to Bardstown Saturday for just one day. "Do you want to go with me?" he asked her. "No," Katie said, "you go and take care of what you need to do and spend some more time with your son." "We will go out Sunday night, anywhere you want to go," she said and hugged him.

Ted left early Saturday and promised to be home early Sunday afternoon. "The next weekend I am home, we will go out to see your family. I haven't seen them for awhile. "I miss the kids," he told her while she was still hugging him.

It was early October before he got back home and that weekend, as he promised, they went to see her family.

Her Mom fixed a magnificent dinner for them. Ted played with the girls and went fishing with her dad and brother. She was happy that Raphael was not there, because she felt guilty about the feelings she had for him the last time she saw him.

The men brought several big fish home. "Told you the first week of October is the best time of the year for the fish to bite," her dad told Ted. He prepared the fish for cooking and her Mom put them in the freezer for another day.

Katie and Ted had a happy two weeks together and Monday Ted received a notice that he had gotten a job in Galesburg, IL. He had ten days before he was to report at the job site. He seemed restless and anxious to get back to work.

He told Katie that he was going home to stay with his son for a few days. Katie had to work and couldn't leave with him, but called him on Friday and asked if he wanted her to drive down and spend a couple of days with them. He answered too quickly that he and Ted Jr. had made plans already that did not include her, but would be home early Sunday.

"What have you been doing all week?" he asked. "I called you Wednesday at work and Ray said you had left early. I called you at home and you weren't there either, were you sick, Katie or out with Mark?"

Katie ignored that question and told him she had gone to the Naval Ordinance office to check out the women's Navy Reserve Program. I thought it might give me something interesting to do with you away so many weekends anymore and she knew the job in Galesburg would be months or maybe over a year. She was hoping he would agree but knew Ted well enough to know that wasn't going to happen.

"What?" he replied loudly, "Now, I guess Mark and I aren't enough for you, you want the whole damn Navy."

"How dare you talk to me like that," Katie responded with anger. "Mark and I have both told you that we never did anything but have dinner together once," she yelled back. "I thought you believed me," she finished.

"I'm sorry, Katie, I do believe you, but you seem to always do the most absurd things when I'm not home." "Why can't you be happy at home waiting for me?" he said more softly this time. You should be getting pregnant, you know I want a daughter," he complained. "Are you doing something to prevent it, Katie?" "No," she answered, "I want a baby, too," but not a girl she was thinking, but my baby Raphael.

"You are all I need sexually, Ted," she told him, "but I have a lot of energy and need more in my life than romance novels." "See you Sunday, Katie," Ted said and hung up.

Early Sunday, Ted came home like he said he would. He walked in the door, kissed her and acted like nothing had happened.

Before she could ask, he asked if she could fix dinner at home tonight. I don't want to go anywhere. Ted read the newspaper he had brought with him and they watched a ballgame on T.V. Around five o'clock, Katie fixed spaghetti and a salad. The sauce was already made and taken from the freezer, so it didn't take long to make the salad, so they were eating early.

After dinner, Ted helped with the dishes, he almost always did, packed his bags for his early morning departure and asked her to come to bed early with him.

"Tonight, you will conceive," he told her. "You can forget about that Navy crap, you will be plenty busy. Then we can get married the first weekend I'm home, O.K., Katie?" he asked.

"We will see, Ted, but if I don't I really do want to join the Reserve and I promise it will not interfere with our life," she said and cuddled up in his arms.

It wasn't long before they were making wild love and forgetting everything else on their minds. Katie fell asleep with Ted holding her hoping all was well with them.

Two weeks went by and Katie had her regular period. She didn't want to tell Ted, but knew she had to because he called everyday and asked.

When she told him, he was no doubt upset and sounded angry.

He missed calling her the next week, so she decided to call him. He never answered his phone, but she knew he had said he would be really busy for the next few weeks and knew he would not be home for awhile.

CHAPTER 18

Katie was sitting by the phone waiting for Ted to call. It was July 1960, Ted had been in Illinois for eight months, he only called occasionally now, but he was coming home tomorrow. Or at least was calling her tonight to tell her if, in fact, he was going to make it.

Her thoughts wandered to the Navy Reserve. She had so wanted to join, but Ted was so against it she never committed herself to doing it. I really do not do much of anything anymore except work and come home, she thought. She didn't even go out to see the kids as often as she used to. She hadn't seen Raphael for over a year and thought how cute he was the last time she saw him.

Ted called and told her he was not going to make it home for another two weeks. I miss you so much, Katie, he had said, but she wondered. She was bored without him but wasn't sure she really missed him anymore.

When he was home, they had a good time together. Their sex life was still good but no longer as exciting. Ted seldom told her he loved her and she knew they would never get married.

The next day when she went into work, she asked Ray if she could take off early Friday, she had decided she would go see Ted if he couldn't come see her.

She loaded her car and six hours later she was in Gaylesburg. She had not called him. She walked through the bar of the hotel.

He was not there. She knew what room he was in because he always told her, so she could reach him in an emergency.

She went to his room and knocked on the door. There was no answer but she thought she heard his voice. Must be on the phone she thought and tried the door.

Her tired eyes popped open and her mouth couldn't speak. The scene in front of her awakened all her tired senses.

There he was in bed, exposing all his gloriously naked backside and under him was a buxom blond favoring Marilyn Monroe, long blond hair falling all over the pillow.

"Katie," he said, and jumped up throwing the sheet over his blond partner, but he knew it was too late. Ted quickly grabbed his underwear and jeans and dressed in record time.

"Ally, get dressed and leave. I will talk to you later," he instructed his bed partner. "This is Katie, my live-in girlfriend back home."

"So, that is all I am to you," Katie whispered. Shock was taking control of her, she began to shake.

Same old Ted, she was thinking as he started pleading with her when Ally left the room. "I'm so sorry, Katie. She doesn't mean anything to me, just a way to pass time until I can get home." "Gets lonely on weekends when I can't come home." "I know," Katie said, "I'm always waiting lonely, but I find something to do besides being unfaithful to you."

"You should have called me," he said, "you should not have driven up here by yourself." "Besides, I know you still see Mark," he accused. "Don't try to blame this on me, Ted." "Be man enough to admit the truth. You are unfaithful to me and no longer respect our relationship." "Don't worry, I'm sorry I broke up your little party, I am leaving to go back home right now." "I'm so sorry that I wanted to surprise you and make you happy." "Seems like I'm the one that got the surprise," she said and actually laughed.

"Don't be stupid, Katie, you can't drive another 6 or 7 hours tonight. Stay here with me tonight and you can drive back early in the morning. Please," he begged.

Katie started out the door and Ted grabbed her arm. "Stop, Ted," she said and pulled away from him, "I'm not sleeping in that bed with you where you were having sex with that woman," and began to cry.

"Then I will get you another room," Ted said and took her in his arms. "O.K.," Katie said. She was too tired and emotional right now to drive.

Ted went to the bathroom to freshen up and told her to wait there while he went downstairs to get her a room. She was too tired to argue. Ted opened the door and watched her as she looked out the window. She looked sad but was no longer crying. "Let's go get your luggage and get you settled in your room," he said gently like he was talking to a child and took her by the hand.

After he got her in her room, he suggested they go out to get some dinner. They went out to eat at a cafeteria near the hotel. While they were eating, Ted begged her not to leave him. "I love you, Katie, that woman means nothing to me." "We will someday have our baby, get married and build a nice house out in the country. I will find a job locally somewhere and never leave you again." "O.K., Katie?" he pleaded with her once more.

"I guess I can stay in my room, but didn't you tell that girl you would talk to her later?" Katie asked him. "That was a lie, Katie. I will never see her again and if it means anything, neither of us climaxed." "She has nothing compared to your beautiful little body," Ted answered, hoping Katie would forgive him.

Katie wasn't sure that she could ever forgive him, but ended up letting him sleep in her room. They made passionate love just as always. "Why would I ever want anyone but you, my beautiful lady?", Ted said and held her close until she fell asleep.

Katie was exhausted and they slept until after ten o'clock Saturday morning. Ted took her to breakfast, they drove around town, went bowling and took in a movie and a late dinner. The night ended with more sex.

Sunday morning, Katie packed up and drove back to Louisville. Ted had promised never to be unfaithful to her again. She hoped that was the truth. She told him she would call when she got home.

CHAPTER 19

Katie had driven home in silence. She had too much on her mind to even enjoy the radio.

She had told Ted she would call when she got home, but decided to see if he would get worried and call her. It was almost eight o'clock. Ted had told her that he was bowling on a Sunday night league from nine until eleven.

Ted never called. She knew he would be at the bowling alley at this time but she would call and leave him a message that she had arrived home late, but safe.

The phone in his room rang, "Hello" Ted answered. He sounded like he was laughing. "Hi, Ted," Katie answered. "I thought you would be bowling, so I was going to leave you a message."

"Why aren't you bowling?" she asked. It was cancelled until next week, he lied, and Katie knew he was lying.

"How stupid do you think I am, Ted?" Katie asked, and I know that girl is there with you again."

Katie had had enough. "This is it, Ted. We are finished," she screamed at him. "We haven't been in love for a long time, you have always resented that I have not gotten pregnant and bore you a child." "Only good sex has kept us together and I don't even want that anymore." "I won't be here when you come home next week or whenever you come home." That was the end of the conversation as far as she was concerned.

"That's not true, Katie, I do love you and you love me, you are just upset," Ted fought back.

Ted knew he had gotten caught again and that made him angry. "You won't leave me, Katie, you are a well kept mistress." Look at you, you never pay any bills, you wear expensive clothes, drive a nice car, live rent-free in a nice apartment and you never pay a penny for any of it. All your money you earn is stacked in the bank or goes to support your family," Ted lashed out at her.

"No, you won't leave me, Katie." "I want you and I know you will be there when I get home, so cool off, honey, and good night. See you next weekend," Ted told her.

"Goodbye, Ted," Katie said and meant just that and hung up the phone.

Katie went to bed and wondered why she wasn't crying. She didn't even feel sad, more relieved and maybe excited about the future.

She had been alone for most of the four years they were together anyway. She was used to making decisions for herself. Her only concern was that she now would be making them on a whole lot less money. She knew she could do it. And now she would be free to join the Navy and that would also help financially. She went to sleep and slept well.

Monday morning she got up early and walked the couple of blocks to the White Castle for coffee and a newspaper before she left for work. She quickly ran through the apartments for rent ads.

She found an efficiency three streets over from where she lived now. She like the neighborhood. She hurried home and called the number for the listing.

"Hello," an older lady answered the phone. "I am interested in the apartment you have listed on Speed Ave. for rent," Katie told the lady. "It is small but very attractive, completely furnished except for a television," the lady added. "And it rents for $15.00 a week." "I have to leave for work now, but I would like to see it this evening at 5:30 on my way home," Katie informed her.

"Yes, that will be O.K., my name is Marjorie Rose and I will send my husband Harold over to meet you there at 5:30."

After introductions, Mr. Rose asked Katie to follow him. The apartment was on the second floor. Katie followed him up the flight of stairs.

When she walked in, it did seem very small compared to her current apartment but it was real cute. There was a small kitchen with brick walls and a bar with stools instead of a table and chairs. The living room was the largest room with a pretty blue couch and two white wicker chairs and coffee table.

Off from the living room was a nice little bathroom with a tub and shower, toilet and a cute sink with a ruffled skirt that matched the shower curtain.

"Where is the bedroom?" she asked. She didn't see any more rooms and there was a big walk in closet on one wall.

Mr. Rose kinda chuckled. "See the white doors with the big handle?" "Yes," she said "What's that?" she asked. He pulled the handle and down came a full size bed, mattress, pillows, covers and all. "That's a surprise," Katie laughed.

She loved the big round window facing the street. It wasn't like her big apartment she was use to, but something she could afford, her present apartment rent had been raised twice since she moved there and she could not comfortably afford it alone anymore.

"I think I will take it," Katie said. Mr. Rose was happy to rent it and told her she could rent it for $60.00 a month or $15.00 each Monday. Also, there was a $15.00 damage deposit. Katie wrote him a $75.00 check.

She was happy that she had made the decision to be on her own. She wondered if Ted would look her up and give her any problems when he got home.

Katie called her Mom and told her that she had broken up with Ted. The whole family was upset with her because they were so fond of him. "Would you have Ron to call me when he gets home?" she asked her Mom.

"Hi," Ron said when she answered the phone. "What's up, Sis?" She explained to him that she was moving and needed his help on Saturday. "You are silly to break up with him, Katie, you have it made," Ron told her. "But I will help you if that is what you want, I will bring Raphael to help too." "Are you sure this is what you want, Katie?" he asked again. "I'm not happy and very seldom see him anymore," she answered. I will pick you up early Saturday morning, O.K.?" "Yes, we will be here waiting for you," her brother assured her.

She hung up the phone and felt like all the blood was draining from her head. She had to sit down. She hadn't seen Raphael for 2 years. He was now 17. She knew she shouldn't see him but couldn't wait until Saturday.

Saturday morning, the guys were at her Mom's waiting for her as Ron said they would be.

"Hey guys," she said when she got out of the car. "Hi," Ron said. "Hi," Raphael said and, of course, was staring at her. Her mind just went blank and she couldn't speak. How could he get cuter every time she saw him, she was thinking.

He was still thin and much taller. His skin was tan and as perfect as when he was a child. And he still had those beautiful eyes that seemed to never blink when he stared at her.

Her Mom and Dad were still upset with her and tried to talk her out of it. But she had made up her mind and no one could change Katie's mind when she had made a decision, right or wrong.

Ron got in the front seat with Katie and Raphael climbed into the back.

Thank God, Katie thought. I don't want to be that close to him.

Ron told her he was getting him a car before Christmas. He and Raphael had been working for Raphael's Dad at Western Union for two summers now and he had saved his money. Raphael told her his Dad had brought him a new Harley Davidson motorcycle but he couldn't have a car until he was seventeen and that meant this year.

After they had moved her television, they stayed and helped her move everything else, her clothes, dishes, linens, everything that she had bought herself. After she was finished, she gave them both $5.00 and took them to Raphael's house.

"We have to all get together," Ron said. "I will come see you more when I get my car." "That will be nice," Katie told him, but she thought he really wouldn't.

CHAPTER 20

R ay had taken the news of her break up with Ted well and told her it would not interfere with their employer-employee relationship. He told her that she did an excellent job and gave her a raise to help with her expenses.

She had not heard a word from Ted and one day asked Ray if he had seen him. "I haven't seen him," Ray told her, "but I have talked to him a few times on the phone." "He wanted to know if you were doing well and if you were happy, said he wondered if you were still working here. He has never asked for your new address, and I never volunteered to give it to him. That is your and his business. Mark has asked for it, but I wouldn't give it to him either," Ray answered her.

Katie never asked about him again. She never saw or heard from him again. Mark had finally come into the store and asked her out to dinner, she refused and never saw him again either.

Katie had been in her new apartment for a year now. Ron and Raphael had kept their promise to visit often. Katie was falling in love with Raphael more every time she saw him.

Ray had also cooperated with her plans to join the Navy Reserve. She took her two week vacation that year to go to Bainbridge, Maryland for her basic training.

For the first few days, it was difficult for her, now 26 years old, to compete physically with the 18 and 19 year olds right out of high school, but after a week, she was participating on equal terms. Academically, she surpassed most of the girls in her unit.

Her body and mind felt like she had crammed four weeks into one. She had experienced long days marching, studying, kitchen duty, and cleaning barracks.

She had flourished in her accomplishments and graduated with honors. She was now wearing her uniform with pride.

She hoped her family and Raphael would be proud of her. Of course, Ron and Raphael were not too keen on the military right now thinking they would be drafted soon as they had 18.

After returning home, she was assigned a yeoman's position at the Naval Ordinance.

She was on duty every other weekend with other Reservists. She loved it and sometimes went to work a few hours when she wasn't on payroll.

On day, she was asked to deliver some forms to the recruiter at the University of Louisville. She wondered if Bob's friend would still be there. He told her he was ready to retire when she had enlisted. He wasn't, an older guy, Randy, who was also ready to retire, had taken his place about five months ago.

After leaving U of L, she drove to Third Street to park her car. Parking on 4th Street was almost impossible at that time of day. She had planned on stopping at Williams to run in to purchase stockings and underwear.

As she was walking on Third Street, she passed Wallace Photo Studio. A bald, middle aged gentleman came running out the door. "Ma'am, we don't see a lot of Navy WAVES around Louisville, only Army." "Would you let me take your picture to put in our window?" "I will give you free photographs," he finished. "Of course," Katie answered, flattered that he would ask her. She had three hours before she had to be back to base and was thinking it would be nice to have pictures in uniform representing four years of her life.

The picture had turned out nice and was displayed in the studio for several years. She kept her small ones and gave the big framed one to her Mom, who proudly hung it over her couch where it remained until her death.

A few guys at the base and others she met in various places had asked her out, but she always turned them down. Men always seemed to complicate her life and she was having so much fun hanging out with Ron and his friends, besides her job and the Navy kept her busy.

One day, Raphael rode his motorcycle to her place. Brought back memories when she rode with him on his little motorbike when he was 14.

He was so proud of his Harley and had to point out every part of it. "Well, are you going for a ride with me or not?" he asked. "Sure, let me get a scarf for my hair," she answered. "No, part of the fun is letting the wind blow through your hair, besides the wind would probably blow your scarf off," he told her.

"O.K.," she answered and climbed on the back of the bike. As soon as she was that close to Raphael, she got the same stirring in her stomach as the last time she was that close to him.

This time it didn't bother her, she admitted she liked being that close to him and really enjoyed the ride. He was right, she could not explain the feeling of the wind rushing through her hair and the feeling of complete freedom like a butterfly soaring into space.

Fall came and it got too cold for the bike. They had ridden every chance Katie got. Now Ron, Raphael, and sometimes their other friends would pile into Katie's car and they would go for hamburgers and cokes and ride around listening to the radio. Katie felt like a kid again.

One Saturday, Ron called and asked if she wanted to go to a movie with he and Raphael and their girlfriends. Katie turned ice cold. She had never thought about Raphael having a girlfriend, and she realized that she was jealous. Thank goodness it was her Reserve weekend, so she had a legitimate excuse to say No.

Monday night, Ron and Raphael came by in Ron's new car to take her out to eat. she was not happy with Raphael but did not want him to know it. She talked mostly to Ron. Raphael was in the front seat with Ron eating his leftover french fries.

After finishing his fries, he threw the empty carton out the car window. Katie yelled loudly at him, "Don't be throwing your trash out on the streets." "Sorry, Katie, stop the car, Ron and let me go pick it up before I get spanked," he said and laughed. "It's not funny, Raphael, that is why our city looks like a dump because of people like you." He looked at Katie with those beautiful brown eyes, clearly showing pain that she would yell at him like that. but he could never get mad at her, not their Katie.

"I am sorry, Katie. I will never do it again," he said sincerely.

When she got back to the apartment and the boys went home or wherever they were going, Katie thought about why she would be so angry about one little piece of paper tossed out a car window.

She was angry with him because it had become a reality to her that he was almost nineteen and, of course, he would have girlfriends.

She refused invitations to go out with them for the rest of the winter. She only saw the boys occasionally. Katie had forgotten the jealous episode also, but she was still very attracted to him.

CHAPTER 21

The spring of 63 had come quickly. Ron and Raphael had both turned 19 and was once again coming to see Katie as often as they could catch her home.

One day Raphael came in alone. "Hi, Raphael," Katie said, "Where's Ron?" "My sister borrowed my car," he explained. "I was with Bobby," "He dropped me off here and Ron is picking me up in a couple of hours, is that O.K.?"

"No plans, Raphael, you are welcome to stay with me," she answered.

Raphael was fascinated with Katie's fold down bed and was talking about it when the phone rang. "Hi, Katie, got to ask a favor of you," Ron was saying.

"Can Raphael spend the night with you?" "My car is broke down. A mechanic at Frank's Garage, where my car is being repaired is taking me home. I will ride back with him in the morning and pick up my car as soon as it is ready and I will pick up Raphael as soon as possible. The guy lives a short distance from me and said he didn't mind. Is that O.K. with you?" he asked. "Sure, he can stay here," she told him. "Let me talk to Raphael," he asked. He must have explained it all to Raphael as he agreed and hung up the phone.

Raphael removed his shoes and socks and then his shirt that he hung over a chair. He was lying on the couch with his tee shirts and jeans on and his feet propped up on one arm of the couch watching T.V. "Got a pillow, Katie?" he asked. "Sure," she said and got him a pillow from the bed. He looked so tall and thin stretched out on her couch and a picture of youthful sex she thought. Stop it, Katie, she told herself. She was as nervous as a deer in the woods at deer hunting season. She sat in the chair and was watching T.V. with him. they watched "I Love Lucy" and a couple more shows he said he liked. "I am going to the bathroom to get ready for bed," she told him. He kept staring at her as he always had. She knew he felt the same attraction as she pulled her bed down and straightened the sheets and went to the bathroom. She could not get him off her mind. He looked so adorable and sexy stretched out on that couch.

Raphael hoped she would come out of the bathroom wearing something short and thin. That would be a site to remember, he thought. About that time, Katie had come from the bathroom wearing a white skimpy silk and lace teddy. Her skin looked at smooth as a baby's behind and those firm little breasts stood up caged in frilly lace. She turned around and Raphael witnessed the cutest butt he had ever seen. It was so round and the teddy so short that both cheeks peeked out just enough to give him a glimpse of what it would look like nude. Her shapely legs ended the pretty picture for him.

His young manhood had grown hard and was pounding his jeans trying to escape.

Katie returned with a small towel in her hand and hung it on a chair close to the bed.

Raphael had already turned off the television. Katie turned the lights out except for a small lamp on the end table.

"Raphael, you don't have to sleep on the couch, you can sleep with me if you want to," she quickly asked him before she lost the nerve.

"Am I getting an invitation I have dreamed about for two years," he asked himself. "My God, will she have sex with me?"

Raphael thought his brains were going to be sucked out of his head. He took his tee off and laid it on the couch. When he slipped his jeans and undershorts off, he noticed his shorts were so wet he wondered if he had peed in his pants.

"What will I do with a woman like that?" he asked himself. She's not a pimple face little teenager in the back seat of a car. God, he thought again, she is a beautiful mature woman and wants to sleep with me. Could I be wrong? Am I making a miscalculation here? he wondered.

As soon as Katie saw his manhood standing straight out in front of him, she wanted to touch it.

When he climbed on the bed beside her, she couldn't wait any longer. She reached over and took it in her hand. It was like a steel rod, wrapped in satin. She almost had an orgasm touching it.

He rolled over on top of her and put his lips on hers. She thought those lips were designed to kiss.

"If you want me, Raphael, you have to undress me," she whispered watching his expressions. "I can do that," Raphael told her in a very nervous voice.

He reached up and pulled one strap off and then the other baring those breasts he had admired under the lace. He touched her breast for a moment before dragging the teddy off her bottom and down to her toes. When completely removed, he threw it on the floor.

Katie spread her legs and he climbed between them. She couldn't wait, she felt the silky head enter her vagina followed by the steel rod. Katie thought she had never felt anything like it. He began to pump it in and out. Katie wrapped her legs around his waist and moved her bottom in rhythm with his strokes. That steel rod was smashing the silky head against her vagina with each stroke. Katie went crazy, so did Raphael. "Katie," he mumbled, "This is a real dream come true." He came long before he wanted to. He had not yet learned to control his penis, it controlled him.

Katie didn't care that it lasted for such a short time, she too had fulfilled a lifelong need for him. She gave him the little towel to clean up with.

"I forgot the condom," he told her, "I'm sorry, I always have one in my wallet." "Don't worry, Raphael, I can't get pregnant," she told him. She had tried with Ted for years.

They didn't talk anymore, they somehow managed to get under the sheets and were both soon sound asleep.

Sometime in the middle of the night, Katie woke with Raphael holding one of her breasts, his hard penis against her back. She flipped over and he was soon inside her again, this time pumping harder and longer. "Raphael," Katie cried out over and over. The explosion happened for both of them together. Katie held him close, she knew she had dug her nails into his back. Wow, she thought, sex with Ted had never been like this. This is how it should always be. Wasn't long before they were asleep again, this time from exhaustion.

When Ron picked Raphael up the next morning, both were fully dressed and eating bacon, eggs, and toast with Raphael's favorite grape jelly. Ron had not eaten so Katie fixed his breakfast also.

"Wasn't too bad sleeping on the couch, huh, Raphael? I have slept there myself."

"Greatest sleep of my life," Raphael replied and smiled at Katie. "Wouldn't dare say anything else," he said and laughed.

The guys got up to leave. "Thanks for breakfast," they both said. "Bye," Katie said, "you are welcome to stay here any night you wish, Raphael."

Damn, that's good news, Raphael thought. The next week was Katie's Reserve weekend. She had worked eight hours there Saturday and would work there Sunday. Raphael had not been over again. She had looked for him every night but he had never been back since.

She got home about 10:30 from her Reserve meeting. When she opened the door, she saw Raphael on her bed asleep. He and Ron both had keys to her apartment.

It surprised her how quickly she was aroused by the site of his naked body asleep on her bed.

She tiptoed to the bathroom, took off her uniform and hung it in the closet, put on a shower cap and enjoyed a fast warm shower. She had used gardenia soap and knew she would smell exciting.

She quietly walked to the bed naked. She barely kissed his lips, then he opened those beautiful brown eyes and looked up at her. "Are you an angel, have I died and gone to heaven?" "No," Katie answered softly, "I'm an angel who is going to take you to heaven for a short time."

She climbed on top of him, put his penis inside her and rode him fast and hard until she was soaking wet. She had an orgasm like she had never experienced before. Each time with Raphael, it was better.

"I love you so much, Raphael, have always," she told him. "Glad you do," Raphael said, but never said I love you too.

When morning came, they showered and dressed and once again Katie fixed him breakfast before she left for work.

Raphael told her thanks, kissed her and left.

I must be the luckiest kid in the whole world he thought. All of he and Ron's friends dreamed of sleeping with Katie. They had no idea what that is like, he thought.

He never told any of his friends about those nights with Katie. They wouldn't have believed him any way.

They would have all loved that experience he knew, but Katie was Ron's beautiful older sister and knew she was off limits. Ron was so protective of her. If any of them had ever suggested anything of a sexual nature about Katie in front of Ron, they knew they would have to pay the price.

Katie had never been so satisfied and loved Raphael more each day. She knew they were matched perfectly. She also knew he still dated other girls, but was contented to be his secret lover.

CHAPTER 22

Katie and Raphael had a hot love affair that lasted all Summer and right into Fall.

One morning in October, Katie woke up sick and ran into the bathroom to throw up. She thought she had picked up an early virus or even worse the flu. She called Ray to tell him that she would not come in. "Take off a couple days, Katie, and get yourself well," Ray told her.

In an hour or so she felt better, must have been something she ate, she thought.

The next morning was a repeat, but after she managed to eat a bowl of cereal and take a shower, she felt better, got dressed and went to work.

After four days of the same scene, she thought about her period. It had been six weeks since her last period. Could she be pregnant? She and Ted had tried to get pregnant but she never conceived in all those years.

Could her prayers for a baby Raphael be answered. If so, he would be a real baby Raphael, one who would look like the little boy she learned to love twelve years ago.

"Yes," she said aloud and felt so happy. Raphael would be over tonight and she wondered if he would be as happy. But Raphael didn't show up that night.

She called Ron and asked why they hadn't been over. "I have been busy," he told her and Raphael is in Florida with his girlfriend and her family."

The next day she went to a doctor who clarified it for real. Suddenly, she was scared and wondered what she was going to do.

She knew she was not going to tell Raphael. She realized he was too young for that kind of responsibility and he proved that their relationship meant nothing to him by going to Florida without even telling her.

She had to call Lisa, she would know what to do. She had married Tom but stayed with the airlines. They lived in a big house right outside Boston city limits.

Lisa had told her at one time that they rented the upstairs to three sailors. Maybe they were no longer there and she could rent their apartment upstairs.

She had so much to take care of. First, she called Lisa. She would not elaborate on her pregnancy, just told her she could not tell the father and needed to leave Louisville. Lisa told her the sailors still lived there, but they had four bedrooms and two baths in their part of the house. "You are welcome to come live with us until the baby comes and you have made permanent plans for the future," Lisa said.

The next day she went into the office and told Ray she would be leaving Louisville in a few days. She told him she was pregnant and could not tell the father just as she had Lisa. He hugged her and gave her a bonus check of $300. "You have been an excellent employee and don't worry about leaving this job. My wife will be happy to come back to work for a while," he said.

She cleaned out her desk drawers, hugged Ray, shed a few tears and left to go to her next stop.

She drove to the Naval Station Personnel Office praying she was making the right decision. She went to the personnel office and filled out forms to transfer to the Reserve unit at Providence, Rhode Island and also a request for two weeks active duty upon her arrival. those two weeks could serve as her two weeks required active duty for that year.

Her last stop was at her landlord's house to give them a three day notice. Just as she thought, they were not happy with that short notice and told Katie that she would not get back the two weeks rent that was already paid. "That's O.K.," Katie told her, "I'm sorry, but it is an emergency and I have to go on Active Duty with the Reserve right away." Mrs. Rose wished her luck and Katie left.

Friday, she packed up her clothes and a few personal items in her four pieces of luggage and took the rest of her stuff to her Mom's to be stored.

While looking into the dresser drawers for things she needed, she found an undershirt of Raphael's that he had left there. She had washed it and put it away and forgotten to give it back to him. She placed it in her luggage thinking of the many nights she knew she would be cuddled up to that shirt, dreaming of its owner.

When Lisa and Tom picked her up at the airport, Lisa hugged her and told her how happy she was to see her. The baby was not mentioned on the way home.

Lisa's home was beautiful just as Katie knew it would be. Her bedroom and bath was mostly pink and very pretty. After she was settled in, Lisa called the three sailors down to meet her, telling them that she was also in the Navy.

They were all nice and offered to take her with them to the base Monday. They explained that they rode a train there and back each day because it was the fastest transportation from Boston.

While Katie was fulfilling her two weeks of active duty at the Naval Base, Lisa was calling everyone she knew working on finding Katie permanent work. About the 6th person called, bingo, that was it. Cliff Arnold owned a Radio Shack on the same side of Boston where Lisa lived and needed a bookkeeper. Perfect for Katie, she told him and would bring Katie over to meet him. Lisa knew Ray would give Katie excellent references and told Katie she knew she had the job if she wanted it. She told her that Cliff was a good friend of Toms so she had nothing to worry about.

Katie started her new job as soon as she had completed her Navy assignment. She had gone to the Women's Hospital in Boston to see a doctor who told her she was due around the 1st of June and everything looked well. Because Katie was single, she told her, she had a choice to abort the fetus but it may be a little late for that she explained and suggested adoption instead. "I want to keep my baby and have every intention of doing just that," she told the doctor who acted surprised. "It is your decision, but it is really difficult for a woman to raise a child without a husband, especially a lady your age," she said to Katie and put her file in a file box on her desk. "Good luck," she said and walked away.

CHAPTER 23

Katie was three months into her pregnancy and was not showing at all. She worried that the baby was still O.K. She went back to the hospital for a checkup, the doctor assured her everything was normal and she would start showing soon.

December in Boston brought a lot of extreme cold and lots of snow. She had left her old Mouton coat at her Mom's and was wearing her fall trench coat.

Lisa was off this weekend and took her to the shopping center near her home to shop for a new coat. She bought a warm camel color wool coat, a brown knit hat, scarf and gloves and Lisa told her she had to buy herself some tall snow boots.

Katie was fortunate that she had brought her savings plus the bonus Ray had given her. She also had the salary from her two weeks reserve duty. She would start getting her pay from her new job in a week, so she did not have a money problem. She had learned to be frugal with her money when she had left Ted. And why would she want to buy many clothes when she would soon be getting maternity clothes anyway. She smiled when she thought of her cute little Raphael inside her.

She loved seeing Lisa and Tom again but she missed her family, Ray, and her co-workers. Personnel at the base were not like her old buddies at the Naval Ordinance in Louisville either. She could not describe the pain of not seeing Raphael. She was so lonely for him and her desire to have him in her bed was overwhelming. She would write him and tell him about the baby and send him a picture after it is born, she thought. Maybe he would then want her also, she dreamed.

Katie had made friends with one of the sailors in the upstairs apartment. He was a tall, good looking blond who told her he was 24 years old.

He would get back from the Naval base each day in time to meet Katie at the subway station and walk the three blocks to their house with her. He told her he didn't think it was safe for a pretty lady like her to be out alone at night in Boston. Katie was grateful to have him to walk with her. She did not like Boston and already wished she was back in Kentucky.

One night, while they were walking home, Keith took her hand. "I have a girlfriend back home in Fruitland, Michigan waiting to get married, I think," he said. "But I am really attracted to you, Katie."

"Keith, I am almost four months pregnant and twenty nine years old," she told him. "I think you are a very nice guy, but I am very much in love with the father of my baby," she added. "Then, where is he?" Keith asked.

"He doesn't even know I am pregnant," she quickly answered in his defense. "He is only 19 and will soon be drafted into the Army. I did not want to burden him with this responsibility," Katie told him and wished he would drop the subject.

"We can be good friends, seems like you could use a good friend right now, do you have medical insurance that will take care of you and the baby's birth?" he asked her seriously. "No," Katie answered. She hadn't thought about that.

The Christmas season came and made Katie even more homesick. She wondered if Raphael was spending the holidays with his girlfriend and if he ever thought of her.

She asked Lisa if she could use her phone to call home and she would pay her when the bill came in. "Of course," Lisa had replied. Katie couldn't wait to get her family on the phone. She talked to her Mom, her sisters, and to Ron, who told her he and Raphael were leaving for the Army next week after Christmas. Katie was so afraid for him and Raphael, Ron was so sure they would be shipped off to Vietnam as soon as they finished basic training.

"Ron," she said, "Please tell Raphael that I am sorry I did not see him before I left, but I had only a few days to report to the Navy base up here. He will understand." "O.K.," Ron said, "he asked where you went so fast. We both miss you he said and gave the phone back to her Mom. She talked with her Mom for a few minutes, told her to give her Dad a hug and reluctantly hung up.

The next day when Keith was walking home with Katie holding her hand as he always did now, he looked down at her and smiled. "We wouldn't want you to fall and hurt that baby girl who looks just like her mother," he said. "No," Katie answered, "it is not a girl, it is a boy who will look just like his father."

"Katie," Keith began, "did you know that you might get a dishonorable discharge from the Navy if they find out you are pregnant and not married?" "I have thought about it," Katie answered him nervously. "You would be honorably discharged if you are married, will you marry me, Katie?" Keith surprised her. "What?" Katie asked, could she not have heard him correctly. "Your baby will be legitimate and have my last name. You could divorce me when your friend gets home from Vietnam, a little older and wiser by then," Keith continued the one way conversation. "I could then marry Terry or someone else."

This guy is weird Katie thought but told him she would think about it.

Three nights later and another proposal, Katie told him, "O.K., Keith, yes, but if Raphael ever comes to get me, I will leave with him." "That's a deal," Keith said and hugged her. "I know that, Katie," he said and squeezed her hand.

Keith told her that he was shipping out in thirty days to serve six months on the U.S.S, Enterprise in the Gulf. We will leave for Michigan as soon as possible and get married before I leave.

He called his Mom and Dad, told them he had gotten this girl (WAVE) pregnant and was coming home to get married before he shipped out. Katie wrote her Mom a letter, told her she was getting married but still did not tell her she was pregnant.

Keith's Mom wanted him to get a test when the baby was born to see if it was really his before he got married.

His Dad told him he was doing the right thing and marry her.

"You are so young, Keith," Tom told him, "Why don't you let Katie stay with us while you are out to sea and decide if you all want to get married when you get back. Lisa and I will take care of her and she can deliver her baby at the women's hospital at the cost she can afford."

But Keith was not going to be swayed. Katie needed someone and he was the guy, he said.

Lisa was disappointed in her leaving her job so soon after she had gotten it for her but told her, she was her best friend and would support her in her decision.

The next day Keith loaded his car with Katie and his belongings, told Tom and Lisa they would stay in touch and started the long trip to Michigan. "Send me a picture of that baby," Lisa said and waved goodbye.

Katie had to pee so much now but was shy in asking Keith to stop for her to go to the bathroom so often. She was in terrible pain when they arrived in Michigan the next morning.

She went into the house with Keith and he showed her where the bathroom was.

Keith's Dad told him what a cute little thing she is. "She looks 16," he said and she hardly looks pregnant. "Can't believe she is already four months."

His Mom, however, said very little to her or about her.

Katie asked Keith if there was some place she could lie down, she was hurting and now getting sick to her stomach. Keith took her to his bedroom and she laid down across his bed. Please God, don't let me lose this baby, she prayed.

The next morning Keith took her to the doctor. She had gotten a bladder infection on the trip.

Three days later she thought she was O.K. She and Keith went to get a marriage license. That is when she found Keith was only nineteen. She said nothing until they were in the car. "Why?" she looked at him. "I thought you would think I was too young as you do Raphael," he told her.

Later that evening a judge whom his Dad knew married them with his Dad and the judge's secretary as witnesses.

Katie had worn her pale blue silk dress and black heels and Keith wore his uniform but because of six inches of snow, she wore her boots and carried her shoes. She didn't know what this wedding would be like so she wanted to look presentable. Of course, it turned out more laughable than the first one.

The Judge explained the marriage vows and Keith put the wide gold band he and his Dad had bought and the Judge looked at them and said, "There you are kids, I will sign your marriage certificate and you are on your way."

Katie had turned 30 yesterday, but his parents thought she had turned 24. Keith's Dad told him he was going to pick up his Mom and meet them at the Steak House to celebrate Katie's birthday and their wedding. Katie still didn't feel one hundred percent well yet and had a miserable time. Keith's Mom kept making funny little jokes about her like she was kidding but Katie knew she meant it.

She kept wondering if she would still sleep upstairs or if Keith would expect her to sleep with him.

When they got home, she was exhausted. It had been a long day. In fact, it had been a trying week for her. "Go on to my room and go to bed, Honey," Keith told her. "I will be there later."

Katie felt the blood drain from her head and she felt dizzy. She must have looked pale. Keith jumped up and grabbed her. "What's the matter, Katie?" he asked. "Just tired," Katie replied and started toward his bedroom.

Why would she think that he wouldn't want to sleep with her, we are married she thought. Keith went to bed with her and put his arm around her. "All this must be very hard for you, my little Katie," Keith said and within fifteen minutes, Katie was sound asleep and dreaming of Raphael.

CHAPTER 24

K eith had four more days at home before he had to report to
Norfolk, Virginia Navel Base to board ship for six months
sea duty.

Katie had not felt well since that bladder infection. Keith, so
far, had been so understanding. He held her at night and never
attempted sex with her. Tonight, he turned over to face her and
asked, "Katie, do you feel like making love tonight?" "I am going
to be out at sea for six months, it is hard for a guy my age to do
without a woman for that long."

"We are married, you know, and that is what married people
do," he pleaded his case.

Katie's heart began to race. She truly thought Keith was the
sweetest guy she had ever met, but she was not sexually attracted
to him.

After sex, he told her she was sweet and beautiful. "Maybe if
Raphael never returns, we can learn to love each other and be a
happy family," he told her. He knew she had not enjoyed the sex
and, frankly, he didn't either. He thought she was a great lady and
wanted to be there for her when the baby came.

Keith was leaving with his Dad to the airport. He hugged
Katie and told her his Dad and Mom would take care of her and
he would write often.

Katie wished she could go home to have the baby. She had not told her family about her pregnancy.

Her father-in-law was very attentive of her. She craved ice cream and he brought her some home every night. That didn't make her mother-in-law very happy. Katie did all she could physically do for her around the house. She always did the dishes and did all the ironing. Sometime she tried to clean the whole house. She felt like she was back in boot camp or even worse, prison. Her mother-in-law just didn't like her.

Eating the ice cream every day, Katie soon began to gain weight. Her father-in- law constantly touched her stomach and sometimes patted her on her backside. She felt so uncomfortable around him and avoided him as much as possible.

By the time April came, Katie was so tired and never felt well. She had begun to have morning sickness again, except it lasted most of the day. She was miserable and wrote Keith and asked if he could possibly come home. Keith had written that he would put in for an emergency leave but it was very difficult to get one when out at sea. Besides, they were one of the ships surrounding Cuba and was expecting trouble.

Keith never made it home in time. On May 4th at 4:30am, Katie woke up soaking wet. Her water had broken while she was sleeping. Her back was aching so bad and she soon began cramping. She had gotten out of bed and put clean sheets and a mattress cover on the bed. She then took the dirty ones to the basement and put them in the washer.

Her cramps were getting worse and she was throwing up again. Her mother-in- law woke up and came to see what was going on. "I'm calling your doctor," she told her and really did sound concerned.

Dr. Koby told her to bring Katie to the hospital immediately.

On the way to the hospital, she thought she felt the baby moving around. She should have felt kicks a long time before but the only thing she ever felt was a little fluttering from time to time.

Dr. Koby was concerned because it was too early for her to be in labor. After examining her and taking blood, he found she still had a lot of infection and was surprised that the bladder infection had not gone away. He told her that she was in real labor but it was too soon and it might not be a good thing for the baby. Katie began to cry. Nothing can happen to my little Raphael, she prayed.

Her blood pressure went up far above the danger figures. The baby was too weak to fight its way out and Katie could not push it out.

She had been in labor for 16 hours. Keith's Dad had called Norfolk and gotten Keith an emergency leave. He was taken to Norfolk by helicopter from ship. He could not get a flight out soon enough so he hitched to Michigan with a truck driver who took him all the way to the hospital and wished him luck.

He was briefed on the situation and allowed in the labor room with Katie. He looked almost as exhausted as she did.

The doctors assessed that the baby was too far down in the birth canal to do a caesarean section and not far enough down to reach with forceps.

The doctor rushed her to the operating room. Katie could barely talk. She heard him tell the nurse, "We have to get that baby out or we are going to lose both of them."

He walked over to Katie and told her he was putting her asleep. They had to surgically take the baby from the birth canal. He could barely get a heartbeat from the baby and Katie's blood pressure kept rising. "Probably too late he said to save the baby but I think we can save the mother", he told Keith.

The nurse gave Katie a shot and she went to sleep.

Katie was cut enough for the forceps to go farther into the birthing canal. He quickly pulled the baby out. He was still alive and started to cry. The nurse quickly took him to the nursery and put him on life-support without cleaning him up.

Once he was breathing on his own, he was cleaned up and dressed in a tiny preemie diaper and undershirt. His birth was recorded at 5:07am on May 5, 1964, but he was not named.

Katie was stitched up and taken to a private room. she woke up and started screaming with pain. Dr. Koby took her hand. "Katie, it is all over and your baby boy is alive. He had been put in an incubator. He weighted 3 lbs. 4 oz., so he has a long way to go to be out of danger but is doing fine at this time."

"You should not be in that much pain now, mostly sore," he said. "I am," Katie cried, "do something." She cried and begged for pain medication. The nurse came in and gave her a shot. "That will do the job, Katie, now get some rest," the nurse said and patted her on the leg.

Katie woke up with the same pain. Dr. Koby decided to take her to surgery to see if something had gone wrong with the forcep birth.

"My son, my son," she kept saying.

Keith was briefed again on the plans to do exploratory surgery on Katie.

She was again taken to surgery, put to sleep and opened up. To everybody's surprise, there was a dead fetus in her tube, must have been a twin. "The bladder infection she was treated for was no doubt an infection in her tube," the doctor told everyone in the operating room. "Her tube must have burst because of the many hours of labor and pushing. She is a very lucky young lady to still be here with us. Without this surgery, she would not have survived another 12 hours."

Keith and his parents listened to the strange story the doctor was telling them.

As soon as Katie was in her room, Keith went in and rubbed her hair. We have a tiny baby boy. Katie and the doctor says you will be completely healed in about six weeks.

Keith had to return to ship. Katie was in the hospital for another week.

She went to the nursery to see her baby every day. He gained a little weight each day and was alert and nursing about 1/2 oz. every feeding about every hour. The hospital kept pressuring her for a name for the birth certificate as soon as he was out of danger and progressing well. Katie named him Mathew Ronald Waqner and called him Matt.

Even after Katie left the hospital, she went back to visit and feed Matt every day. She loved holding him. He was so tiny and sweet.

He had blue grey eyes like her Dad, but he would stare at her just like his Dad, the same unblinking expression.

On June 2nd, the hospital called and told her that Matt had made it to five lbs. and was ready to go home. The nurses cried when she took him. They said he had been their baby for a month.

Katie never realized it was going to be so hard. It was difficult taking care of a preemie. She was up night and day for a month.

Both she and baby got stronger every day. In the middle of July, she wrote Keith and told him she was planning on a trip to her parents. She had called them and told them when Matt was born and the details of why he was so tiny. She told them he was premature, so they never suspected he was not her husband's. At least, if they did, she never ever knew it.

Ron and Raphael were finally drafted and were leaving for Vietnam in a couple of weeks and she wanted to see them before they left. She was planning on telling Raphael about his son.

CHAPTER 25

Katie's father-in-law took her to the airport and told her to have a good time. She was so excited to be going home, she had not seen her family since last October. Ron and Raphael were both home for the weekend and Ron was going to pick her up at the Louisville airport. She had written to Raphael and told him she would call him when she got home and hoped they would see each other soon. Raphael knew she had a baby boy but still did not know the child was his.

The baby had slept most of the flight home. She had a slight layover in Detroit at which time she fed and changed him before time to board the plane for Louisville.

The plane trip reminded her that she had never sent a picture of the baby to Lisa. She felt guilty and promised herself that she would do it as soon as she returned to Michigan.

Her family was happy to see her and, of course, the baby. Everyone commented on how tiny he was.

She visited with her family for a couple of hours and asked her Mom if she would mind if she called and ask Raphael over for awhile before dinner.

"Of course not, we would love to see him too," she said.

His sister answered the phone. "He isn't home but I will tell him you called when he gets home," she said. Katie was disappointed. "Tell him I am at Ron's house," she responded.

Fifteen minutes later Raphael called her back. "Hi Raphael, do you want to come over to Mom's for a bit?" "I want you to see my baby."

"Be there in a few," he answered. Katie was excited and thought Raphael sounded excited too.

His car pulled into the drive about ten minutes later. Katie's hormones went crazy. He walked in and gave her a hug. He looked the same except his hair was clipped close to his head, but those beautiful dark brown eyes were the same she noticed as he stared at her.

He talked to her Dad and Ron for awhile about he and Ron's orders to Vietnam, about when they were kids and he had stayed with them most of the summers, and Raphael's car, a sixty Chevy Impala.

He walked over to Katie, "How have you been, young lady?" "Busy with a new baby," Katie answered. "Do you want to see him?" she asked. "Sure, what's his name?" Raphael asked. His name is Mathew. I call him Matt." Ron looked surprised but said nothing, Mathew was his brother's name.

Katie went into the bedroom to get him. He was awake and grunting for a bottle. She took him into Raphael. "Do you want to hold him?" Raphael squirmed a little and said, "No, Katie, he is too little. Maybe when he gets older and a little bigger," he answered and smiled.

"Katie, would you like to go out to eat dinner with me? You can bring the baby," Raphael asked. I would like that," she answered. Her Mom told her to go on out for awhile that she would enjoy keeping her new grandson. Katie instructed her Mom where everything was in the diaper bag and told her he was ready for a bottle right now.

Raphael opened the car door for Katie and then got in himself. "Where do you want to go?" he asked her. "Don't care," Katie said. "I was thinking the Kingfish," he suggested. "That's O.K.," Katie said.

As soon as they left the driveway, Raphael looked over at her and asked, "Why did you run away so fast when I was in Florida?"

"I would have come back to you, Katie, I missed you," he finished. Those expressive brown eyes looked sad." "Because," Katie began, "I was pregnant with your baby, you were in Florida with another girl and I knew you were too young to face that kind of responsiblity," she felt sad too.

"So he is my baby." It was more of a statement than a question, so Katie offered no more.

They had a good dinner at the Kingfish and Raphael asked where she wanted to go. "Somewhere where we can be alone," she said. "Will you go to a motel with me, Katie, there is a Holiday Inn right down the street?" Katie nodded yes.

They drove in silence to the motel. Raphael went in and got a room. She followed him inside and returned to the car to get Kate.

When they were inside, Raphael came over and put his arms around her. "When I came back from Florida, I missed you and felt that I had meant nothing to you." "I had gone to Florida with Pam to break up with her. I knew I would be leaving for the Army soon. I wanted to be with you as much as I could before I left."

"Oh, Raphael," Katie sobbed. "I didn't know, I thought I meant nothing to you."

She put her arms around his neck and pulled him to her. He kissed her a long sexy kiss. "I want you," she sighed. I have missed you making love to me." "Are you sure?" Raphael asked.

"Yes," Katie said, "I left you because I loved you, I still do and will forever." "Do you want to go to bed with me, Katie?" he asked her. "Yes," Katie said without hesitation.

They both undressed and climbed in bed. Raphael was holding her slightly touching her breast. He put his hand on her butt and pulled her closer. "Never could forget this cute little ass," he said. Their kisses got hotter. Raphael sucked her lip while his tongue explored every inch of her mouth. He straddled her and spread her legs. He touched the soft little ball of hair protecting the prize he was searching for. Parting the hair with his thumb, he found the little knob. Katie went wild squirming beneath him, his manhood knocking against her trying to get in.

Raphael kept asking her "What do you want, Katie? What do you want? Katie cried out "You, Raphael, you, I can't wait any longer, I want you inside me." Raphael slid it in slowly. Raphael, Katie said, "I have missed you, I love you so much!" Raphael was moving now faster and harder. Katie was holding him so tightly. She couldn't control her emotions and didn't want to. She had waited far too long for him.

"Raphael," Katie was begging. "Don't ever stop, don't ever leave me again."

Katie felt like she was flying, stars twinkling all around her. Both climaxed the same moment. Raphael fell back on the bed beside her soaking with sweat, the sweet emotions draining from his body.

He turned over and held her in his arms. How is it there is no other woman that can satisfy me like this woman, Raphael was thinking.

Katie hugged him and started to cry. "Please Raphael come back from Vietnam," she begged. "I can't live without you." "Let's enjoy the time we have now," Raphael told her and kissed her mouth over and over.

They stayed in bed for an hour and talked. "I can drive you back home Wednesday," he told her. "that will give me four days before I have to report to the base for departure." "Maybe if I'm lucky I will get more of this little angel," he said and winked at her.

They made love again, this it time it was even more possessive, more demanding of each other. Katie knew she was going to literally explode with love and feelings she had for him. She felt like she would die when he left her. She had held him until her arms ached.

Finally, on the ride back home, she had to ask, "Raphael, do you want me and our son?" Keith told me that he would divorce me if you wanted your son," she told him and watched his eyes for an answer. "He married me to avoid some problems I would have had, having the baby unmarried," she tried to explain her marriage to Keith as Raphael listened.

Raphael was quiet for a few minutes. "Katie, I am going to Vietnam. Chances are slim that I will ever return. Hundreds of men are killed over there daily. Go back to your husband, he can give you a home, he will give your son a father. I can't give you anything right now," he finally finished.

"I will write you if you want me to," he said, "and maybe come see you when or if I ever return." "I will always love you, Raphael. I will always belong to you, body, heart, and soul," she told him tears running down her face.

"By the way, Katie, I watched you undress, you don't look like you had a baby, you are still beautiful," he said in a lighter tone, trying to change the subject.

When they got to the house, he did not go in, just dropped her off. "See you tomorrow, Katie," he said and waved goodbye as he drove away.

Raphael was taking her back to Michigan early Wednesday morning. That gave Katie two more days at home.

When Raphael called her Monday morning, she told him she needed to stay with her family the next two days, but that she would go for a ride with him at night.

Monday was a fun day for her with her sisters and Mom. Matt began to smile a little and everyone wanted to hold him. Monday night Ron and Raphael took her to a movie as Grandma wanted the chance to babysit again. They had fun just like they did a few years ago. Raphael treated her as Ron's big sister just like he used to.

Tuesday night, Raphael came to dinner. It was Ron's last night at home before reporting to base to leave for Vietnam.

Immediately after dinner, Ron left for his girlfriend's house. Once again, Katie asked her Mom to keep Matt while she and Raphael went for a ride. Raphael wanted to drive to the Deer Horn Lake where they went as kids.

They parked near the lake and walked down to the edge of the water holding hands and talking about times Katie would load all the kids in her car and come here to play. "Seems like only yesterday," Raphael said. "Seems like someone else to me," Katie replied.

They returned to the car and Raphael pulled her to him and kissed her. They ended up making love in the back seat of his car.

Wednesday morning brought tears for Ron and Raphael. Her Mom and Dad were so sad. Her Mom clung to Ron as he went out the door to the waiting car, a friend driving him to the base. They also cried when they told Raphael goodbye knowing they would not see him again before he left next week. They were sad to see her and the baby leave also. "Come back soon, Katie," her Mom begged. "We miss you living so far away." "I will come back here to live one of these days," she promised her Mom, thinking when Raphael came back they would get married.

Katie called her in-laws to see if they had heard from Keith. "In fact, he surprised us when he walked through the door yesterday. The Cuban crisis had died down and he was sent stateside early," her father-in-law told her. "Wait, you can talk to him."

Keith came on the phone. "Are you having a good time with your family, Honey?" he asked. "Do you want me to pick you up at the airport, what day are you coming home?" "I'm coming home today, Keith, but not flying. Raphael is driving me home to save a little money if that is O.K. with you." "Sure," Keith said, always good to save money and I would like to meet him. Sorry about your brother."

Keith explained to his parents that a friend of Katie's brother was bringing her home and that they had been friends for a long time.

"Keith is happy that you are bringing me home," Katie told Raphael. "Yea, I bet," Raphael said. He thought she was a little nuts but Katie was Katie and he always listened to Katie his whole life.

When they arrived at her in-laws, Keith came out to meet Raphael. They talked to each other about the war and the Army versus Navy.

Keith's Mom fixed them all sandwiches and a glass of milk. Katie's father-in- law told Raphael he was welcome to spend the night, but Raphael insisted that he was going to a motel and driving home early in the morning. He made the proper goodbyes including Katie. He didn't hug her but patted his baby on the head.

When Katie and Keith went to bed, it felt strange to her. Her heart was breaking for Raphael and thought of him all alone in that motel. She wondered if he was thinking of her. She wished!

Keith turned out the light and turned to Katie. "I guess he doesn't want you or his baby either, huh?" he asked.

"Of course, he does," Katie said in Raphael's defense. "He is going off to war and thinks he won't return." He says you will take good care of us."

She was sad but thought he would be back and come back and get her and Matt then.

After Raphael was in Vietnam for a couple of weeks, Katie called his Dad and got his address. She wrote him often and sent him pictures of Matt and sometimes herself. Once in awhile, he would write her back. He seldom said anything about his son but would tell her that he missed her, but never said he loved her.

Once, he mentioned how after she had left for Boston, he would walk down Third Street past Wallace Studio to see her picture in the window. "I missed you," he wrote.

Keith had been discharged from the Navy, got a job as a city policeman and bought a house. Matt had grown into a cute very blond toddler and looked just like his Dad.

Katie and Keith had grown closer and were great friends, but definitely not lovers. They seldom had sex, only when Keith had been drinking a lot. Katie thought he was drinking far too much with his friends, but he had drank a lot when they were in Boston also, so she didn't think it too far out of character for him.

August 3, 1965, Katie had put Matt in his playpen when she heard a car pull in the drive. She knew it wasn't Keith, the motor sound was too powerful.

She looked out the window to see a beautiful red Corvette sitting in the driveway. The door opened and out stepped Raphael.

Katie ran out the door and jumped upon him almost knocking him down. Tears of joy were running down her face. "Raphael, you did come back," Katie said not knowing if she meant from Vietnam or back to her. "I got in late last night and stayed at a motel," Raphael said as he was hugging her.

"Come in," she said and held on to his arm as they went into the house. "Where is Keith?" Raphael asked. "He will be back in a few minutes," she said.

"He went to put gas in the police cruiser." "Come on in and see how Matt has grown. He is 15 months old and looks more like you everyday," Katie told him.

Raphael walked over to the playpen and patted him on the head, "Hi, little fellow," he said but did not pick him up. Matt was not sure of him and reached up for Katie to pick him up.

Keith came home and was happy to see Raphael. He had one more errand to do and asked if Raphael wanted a ride in the cruiser. Raphael thought that would be fun and went with him. Keith showed him everything in the car. They talked about police work, Vietnam, and girls, of course. Both guys were definitely girl watchers and had fun together. Keith was on night shift but had been off the day before and didn't feel like he had to sleep all day.

When they got back, it was Raphael's turn to take Keith for a ride and show off the Corvette.

It was getting late in the afternoon when they returned. Katie had cooked dinner and Raphael ate like he was starving. After dinner, Keith had to get ready to go to work.

Raphael watched television while Katie cleaned the kitchen and give Matt his bath. Racial riots dominated the news across the South. Raphael commented on how some cities looked like war zones.

Later, Raphael asked if he was sleeping on the couch or if she had a guest room. "Don't be silly, Raphael, you can sleep with me," she told him. Raphael was surprised, but didn't argue with that. "I'm tired now, he said.

Katie put Matt to bed and led Raphael to her bedroom. When he took off his shirt, she noticed he had gotten skinny again.

The minute he touched Katie, he became hard. Wasn't long before they were into the hot love making as usual. Sex seemed magical for them.

After exhausting each other, she laid in his arms and they talked.

"I knew you would come back for me," Katie said and kept on kissing his sexy sweet tasting mouth.

"I can't take you back with me now," he told Katie. "I don't have a job yet, only money I saved while in the service, I spent a hunk on the Corvette." "I am living with Mom and Dad." "Maybe you can send for me when you get more settled," Katie said. "We'll see," Raphael answered. Raphael held Katie close to him while she slept, but he did not sleep much.

At six o'clock, Matt woke up. Katie slipped out from under Matt's arm and went in to get the baby. He always got hungry about the time for Keith to get home in the morning.

Keith came home and asked where Raphael was. "Asleep in our bed," she told him. Keith knew they had slept together. "I will go to the guest room and go to bed," he said. He picked up Matt and gave him a hug and went upstairs to the guest room. "You are going back with him this time, aren't you?" he asked as he was walking to the stairway.

"No, I'm never going to go with him," Katie told him sadly. Keith looked at her and answered, "That's O.K., Katie, you will be O.K." She looked so sad and he felt sorry for her. He gave her a stern look and said. "Either now or never. Matt will be getting older and he needs only one father, I will tell him before he leaves," Keith said and disappeared up the stairs.

Raphael got up and Katie fixed him breakfast, "You know that I will always love you, Raphael," she told him while he was eating. "I know that, Katie," and gave her arm a gentle pinch.

Raphael wanted to take Katie somewhere in the Corvette before he left as planned the next morning. Katie got Matt ready and herself. They decided to drive to Grand Haven to see the musical fountains.

When they arrived home, Keith was awake. Katie started to fix dinner. "Do you have a McDonald's in this town?" Raphael asked. I have missed the great American hamburger, don't have those things in Vietnam," he said and laughed. "Sure," Keith answered. "I will treat if you will take us in your car." "That vet won't hold us all," Raphael said. Keith agreed. Katie won't have to cook. They all went to McDonald's for burgers and fries, just like old times with Raphael and Ron, Katie thought.

"Take me for one more ride in the Corvette, Raphael, will you?" Keith asked Raphael when they got back home.

When they returned, Raphael was very quiet. Keith went to work. "See you in the morning," he told Raphael before he left. But after Keith left, Raphael told Katie he was going home, he decided it would be faster to drive all night instead of driving in all the morning traffic.

Katie clung to him crying. "I will come back soon," he told her. But Katie knew he didn't mean it. He kissed her goodbye and said, "I love you, Katie," and got into his car and left. He never even looked at his son. Katie knew she would probably never see him again. She cried herself to sleep.

CHAPTER 26

The years went by quickly. It was Feb. 1981, Keith and Katie had just celebrated their 17th wedding anniversary. They were never a happy couple but not an unhappy one either.

After Keith's short lived affair with his ex-fiance the second year of their marriage they silently committed themselves to be loyal to their exceptional friendship and raise their son together.

The first five years of their marriage had sometimes fun. They went out a lot as a family and took Matt to every event in Michigan geared for children.

But they seldom went out as a couple with the exception of the police department social events.

Keith went out occasionally with his male friends to drink or play poker. Katie would stay home with her son or take him out somewhere to play.

The first five years Katie was married, she lived in Michigan and drove to Kentucky most every weekend after Matt was a year old. After he turned six, she decided she was going to move back to her home state. She had told Keith of her plans. He did not want Katie to leave him and arranged a transfer from his city patrolman job to the Kentucky State Police, with only a brief period of unemployment.

When Katie's brother Ron had come home from Vietnam a heavy drinker and drug user. He and Keith had bonded like brothers and were almost inseparable.

About 1975, Keith began to wander away from his lifestyle with Katie and Matt. He seldom saw Matt and Katie was usually in bed when he got home at night. Katie knew he had multiple affairs over the years and had moved into her own bedroom, but somehow she and Keith had remained close friends. Katie knew she would always care for him and felt that he needed her now that he was an alcoholic just like she needed him years ago when she was pregnant.

One evening, in 1981, Keith was sitting at the kitchen table drinking his last six pack of beer before going to bed and Katie was ironing his work shirts. He was no longer a patrolman but was still with the state working a desk job at the post headquarters.

The phone rang and Keith answered it. He asked the caller, "What happened, when?" He laid the phone down on the table. He got up and put his arm around Katie, "Katie, sit down," he told her. She was alarmed because he had turned so pale and seemed to sober up instantly.

"Are you sick, Keith?" She then put her arm around him. "No, Ron is dead," he blurted out and held her and began to cry. "What?" Katie asked again. "Keith, what are you trying to tell me?" Keith repeated, "Ron is dead, he was killed in a car accident early this morning."

"No, no, no, don't say that Keith, how much have you been drinking?" Katie said, not wanting to believe him.

"Get the phone," he said. Alice is on it. Katie had forgotten that he had just laid it down on the table. She grabbed up the phone, Alice was still on the other end crying. Alice repeated the story to her that he was killed in a car wreck around 4a.m. that morning.

Katie hung up the phone, put up her ironing and went into the bedroom where Keith had vanished while she was talking to Alice.

They both held each other and cried until they could not cry another tear.

The next couple of days were a horrible nightmare for Katie. She tried to console her parents, cope with her teenage son's reaction to the tragedy and keep Keith sober for the funeral.

Somewhere amidst all the grief, she thought of Raphael. She supposed she should call him, since he and Ron were so close growing up and like brothers before Vietnam.

She remembered several years ago that Ron had told her Raphael had moved to Atlanta and got married. She had felt betrayed and for the first time since the birth of her son, realized that he was not coming back to her.

She called long distance and asked for the number of Raphael Willis. It rang and Raphael answered the phone. "Hello," he said in a familiar voice except for an octave lower.

"Hi, Raphael, this is Katie," she could barely get the words out of her mouth because the chills and violent shaking was preventing her from continuing the conversation.

She tried to get control. Raphael was still talking, "Where have you been, Katie?" "I didn't know where you lived and Ron and I lost contact when we returned from Vietnam." "Nice to hear from you. I'm married now." He seemed to rattle on without breathing. "How is Keith and your son doing?" he continued.

Katie finally was able to speak and interrupted. "Ron is dead." "What?" Raphael asked after she finally got his attention. "He was killed in a car accident yesterday. He was a heavy drinker and passed out driving. He hit a tree." "Oh, no," Raphael said and became silent again.

"The funeral is day after tomorrow," she said. "My wife and I will leave for Louisville this evening. Where can I call you when we arrive?" Raphael answered. Katie was wishing she hadn't called but gave him her phone number and told him goodbye. Her thoughts were racing through her mind at the speed of lightning. What was she going to do, she still loved him and couldn't stand to see him with another woman, especially a wife. What was she thinking!

The next morning Raphael called and told her they were at the Best Western Motel near her and wanted to know where the funeral was going to be held. He told her, he and Sandy would attend the funeral but could not go to the cemetery. He said he would have to be back to work the next day.

Raphael was wearing jeans and a navy blazer with a shirt and tie. That was the first time Katie had ever seen him in a tie. His hair was cut short and she noticed he was still skinny but not tanned as she remembered him. He did not look older just more mature. My goodness, he is now 36, Katie thought.

Katie and Keith got out of the car and walked over to them. Katie looked him directly in the eyes but for the first time ever, he averted his eyes away from Katie's face. He introduced his wife as Sandy, she thought. Katie never acknowledged the introduction.

Raphael reached out and hugged her. His touch was like a painful torch burning her insides to the pulp.

Thank you for coming, Raphael," she said and turned and walked away. Raphael and Sandy sat somewhere in the back of the church. Katie was in the front with Matt and Keith.

After the service was over, Katie went up to the casket once more and Keith went outside. Raphael went up to him and told him again how sorry he was and that the memories of he and Ron's childhood together would always be in his heart. "Please tell Katie bye for me," he told Keith, "We are leaving." He never mentioned his son.

Katie thought he did not want to see the pain in her face to haunt him for the rest of his life. I know he knows how much I still love him, she added to her thoughts.

She cried for her losses for days. How could she have lost her brother and the only man she would ever love within the same day.

Keith told her that he could see how hurt she was and also how stupid she had been for years. "I will always love him, Keith," she said, "but I will never see him again or even tell anyone that Matt is not your son."

CHAPTER 27

After Ron's death, Keith drank more and more often. He was a functional alcoholic and was capable of performing the eight hours at work before he started his nightly drinking ritual.

Thanks to the guys at the Police Post who helped Katie get a job in the prison system, she was making a decent salary and could keep up the household bills.

She was working long hours, sometimes more than fifty hours a week. She saw very little of Matt and seldom saw his father sober. He got with the pot smoking crowd and Katie lost all control of him.

At one time, Keith was having an affair with a school teacher and decided to move in with her. After three weeks, he came home begging Katie to let him come back. He promised Katie that he would quit drinking and never have another affair. He claimed he was sorry for all that he did not do to help Matt stay on the right track.

Katie did allow him to come back home but, of course, the promises were soon forgotten.

Matt was a high school senior and was doing better. Katie had bought a nice house in a good neighborhood and he seemed to be maturing until one day the door bell rang.

A pretty tiny little blond girl asked if Matt was home. "No," Katie said. The young lady began to cry. "Come in," Katie said.

She put her arm around the girl and asked her why she was crying. "Has Matt gotten into some kind of trouble?" she asked. "What is your name sweetheart?" Katie remembered to ask.

"My name is Kim Langdon," and I'm pregant. The baby belongs to Matt and he knows it but won't talk to me unless I tell him I will have an abortion," she told Katie. "And I don't have the money for an abortion and Mom and Dad don't know I'm pregnant."

"Besides, I love Matt and I don't want to have an abortion. I want to get married and have the baby."

"How old are you, Kim?" Katie asked thinking she looked 16. "I'm 18," Kim told her. "I turned 18 last week." "How pregnant are you in terms of months or weeks," Katie questioned. "Eight weeks, I think," Kim told her not really sure. She had not been to a doctor and was afraid to tell her parents.

"Tell you what, Kim, your parents will find out soon, let's you, I and Matt go talk to them. I will help you with your medical bills and Matt can get a job when he gets out of school. You go on home now and I will talk to Matt when he gets home. Don't worry, Honey, we will work it out together."

Katie was upset with Matt that he would do that and then not even talk to the girl.

When Matt got home, Katie accosted him immediately with what Kim had told her and asked if he was sure the baby was his.

"Yes," he responded quickly, "but I am not going to marry that girl or anybody at 18 years old. Besides you think I'm bad smoking pot, before she got pregnant, she was smoking and popping pills. She is just pretty to look at and good for sex."

"O.K.," Katie told him, "but you have to take some kind of responsibility. Kim is coming over today and I want you to be home. We are all three going to her parents and let them know we will do all we can to help her."

"Sure," Raph said and got up and walked out the door.

When Kim arrived, she was crying again. "I saw Matt at the drugstore, but he pulled out of the parking lot when he saw me walking over to the car," she managed to get out between sobs.

Katie was about to tell Kim she would go with her to talk to her parents when her phone rang. "Hello," Katie said. "Is this Matt's Mom?" the lady on the other end of the phone practically screamed. "Yes," Katie said, "This is Katie, what can I do for you?" Katie's intuition told her who she was talking to. "You can kill that bastard son of yours," she said in a hostile tone. "Could we talk about this in a civil manner, Kim is already pregnant and she needs our support now, I didn't realize she had told you yet, she is here now, we don't live too far from you, could you come over and we all talk?" Katie asked in a very quiet dignified manner. She thought this lady was very ignorant or very arrogant. "My husband and I will be there in about a half hour," she asked for the address.

When they arrived, the husband introduced them to her and the wife simply glared at her like she had been responsible for Kim being pregnant.

They made it very clear to her that Kim was not having an abortion but would give up the child for adoption at birth.

Katie told them she and Matt would pay for half the medical expenses. Her father told her that his insurance would pay for her expenses but I want the assurance that your son will never go near her again or attempt to see the baby when it is born. They looked at Kim and told her to come home immediately and left without another word to Katie.

After they left, Kim thanked her for being nice to her and left because she had to, Katie began to get mad. She felt that Kim's parents had been rude to her and their daughter.

Damn, Katie thought, that's my grandchild. We will see about that child being adopted by strangers. When Matt gets home, he had better listen to me or I will beat a little sense into him. I'm tired of him disrespecting me and walking away when I am talking to him.

It was after nine when Matt got home. Katie was sitting in the kitchen drinking coffee. Keith had gone to bed an hour ago drunk. Matt came into the kitchen and poured himself a glass of milk.

"Sit down, Matt, I need to talk to you." Katie pointed at the bar stool where she meant for him to sit. "Now what," Matt asked. "We have to do something to prevent Kim from giving her baby up to strangers," Katie started.

"I'm not marrying that broad no matter what she does," he began. "Look, Matt, you may not want it now, but in the future, you will always wonder if you have a son or daughter out there somewhere." "A baby is the most precious thing in the whole universe. I loved you more than life the day you were born and I love you now. Listen to Mom just this once," Katie begged. "You have no idea how special you are," Katie told him and Matt thought she had a wild look on her face like she was talking to him but she was far away. Of course, Katie was thinking of Raphael.

"I'm going to bed," Matt said, "tomorrow is a school day, now don't go and do something stupid." He got up and kissed her on the cheek and went upstairs. The next day, Kim came back over and asked Katie if she could stay there, her Mom had told her to leave and not come back until she agreed to give up that heathen child. "I want my baby but I don't know how I would take care of it," she mumbled through her crying again. "Don't cry, Kim, you have to go home and tell your parents that you are thinking about it, give me a little time, I will think of something," Katie was actually thinking out loud.

That evening at dinner, she approached Keith and told him her plans. Matt thought she was crazy but agreed to it as long as he did not have to take any responsibility for the child's care.

The next day, she checked her savings account, emptied it, and went to a local attorney. Matt was to contest the adoption as the father and agree on his parents adopting the baby.

Thank God fate was on her side. The judge ruled that the child was better off with grandparents and father than with strangers.

Katie had a beautiful granddaughter born on her birthday. Kim held her and thought she was beautiful. Matt pretended he didn't care but kept talking about how cute her soft duck down hair kept blowing about her head.

When she took baby Karla home, she nicknamed her Karley Bug which little Karley never quite outgrew at home. Katie told Kim she could come see her anytime she wanted but that she would make all the decisions in her upbringing. At first, Kim came to see her often but within 6 months, she had a new boyfriend and came less and less. Matt sometimes would talk to her when he was home but he mostly ignored her.

Katie had taken six weeks off from work and after that would get a sitter. She knew she would have to go back to work. She also knew the job and a baby would be challenging at 49, but she knew she could do it.

Keith loved Karley Bug and she loved him. He actually cut down alot of his drinking. He was so happy with Karley Bug and treated her like she was his. And the lonely void in Katie's life was once again filled by a child.

As Karley Bug grew, she excelled at school, on dance teams, and beauty pageants. She was Miss State Co-ed when she was a Freshman in college.

After completing college, Karla, as she was now called married a computer company CEO and had three beautiful children of her own. Katie was as proud of her great grand children whom she called her grand children as she was Matt and Karla.

Matt had gotten married but did not have any more children. Kim was in and out of Karla's life but Katie was happy that Karla knew her parents. She and her Dad had gotten close as he got older.

Keith was lonely again and missed Karley Bug as she grew older and went back to his garage drinking all day as he did twenty years ago.

Katie was now 68 and worked only part time. She was happy that she had Matt and Karla and the kids in her life. She hadn't had time to be lonely for years.

One day when she was cleaning, she found a box of old pictures stuffed away in a closet. She sat down in the floor and was enjoying the pictures of her parents and siblings years ago. She found a picture of Ron sitting on a rock when he was two and felt sad for a moment and school pictures of the girls that made her laugh. She remembered all the good times she had with the kids when she would go home on weekends years ago.

At the bottom of the box was a picture lying face down. She picked it up and turned it over. Her insides turned to mush. It was a picture of Raphael when he was eighteen.

She hugged the picture to her racing heart and big tears rolled down her cheeks. "Where are you, Raphael?" she asked aloud. "Don't you know that I still love you? Are you still alive?"

She took the picture to her bedroom and put it under her pillow. When she went to bed, she held it to her heart remembering his young body, his male smell, the sound of his voice telling her that he would have come back to her from Florida if she had just waited.

Her body ached for his sweet and wild sex and her dreams that night were confusing. She would wake up sweating knowing he was in her dream but could not remember the dream.

The next morning she put the picture back in the box where it would not be seen again for years.

28
CHAPTER

Katie came home from work to find Keith passed out on the garage floor. Blood was coming from a wound on his forehead. She immediately called 911 and felt for a pulse. She could not find one, but when the EMS arrived, the lady said she could find a weak one but that he had lost a lot of blood and was getting weak.

Katie followed the ambulance to the hospital emergency room where his wound was stitched up and then assigned a room.

After he was assigned to his room, he was then taken for a CT scan and other tests.

Katie stayed with him overnight. She had called Matt and Karla. They both had come to the hospital but both had to leave around 10 o'clock. Matt had to go to work the next morning and Karla had to go home to the kids.

Early the next morning, the doctor came into the room and ask Katie to step out into the hall.

"Mrs. Waqner, when the head scan was done, we found a tumor in Keith's throat," he told her with much concern in his voice.

"I will order a biopsy today. We are quite sure it is cancer," he told her. "He says he is a heavy drinker and will try to convince you to let him go home," Dr. Lee told her but we will keep him sedated so he will sleep alot.

Katie was really scared. Alice had died of cancer 12 years ago and now she was afraid she would lose her dear friend and husband of 46 years.

The biopsy proved it to be throat cancer. Keith was to stay in the hospital for a week before surgery to restore the blood he had lost and to give him the proper nutrition he needed. He was fit to be tied. He missed his alcohol and cigarettes.

Karla and Matt were told the truth and that he would have surgery next week. Karla cried and screamed, "My Granddaddy, why him?" the old closeness of she and her grandfather when she was a child came flooding her thoughts. She stayed by his side as much as she could.

Matt would come in every other day. He was pensive for days, just hugging his Dad and one day started to talk to him like he was a child telling him things they were going to do together when he got out of the hospital.

After Keith recovered from the surgery, he started chemo treatments that made him ill and radiation that burned his throat raw. He could no longer eat and was fed through tube feeding for a while. But Keith was never a whiner and took it all like the man he was. He was determined to beat it.

One day, Katie caught him drinking beer in the garage. She called Dr. Lee and asked if it would hurt him with the chemo treatments. Dr. Lee said he was surprised that he could drink it but it didn't much matter as the cancer was in Stage Four and spreading.

He never much improved. Katie took off from work to nurse him at home for as long as she could. He was beginning to fall a lot and Katie had trouble getting him up. The next CAT Scan showed the cancer was entering the left side of his brain.

Katie called Hospice and made arrangements for him to go to their unit in the hospital.

Keith begged her not to let him go, he wanted to die at home.

Once he fell and broke two ribs. Sometimes he didn't know who Katie was. Katie knew he needed stronger pain medication and had to be hospitalized to get it.

The second day he was in the Hospice Care unit, he acted much better and actually talked to Katie like he was improving.

Katie was sitting by his bed holding his hand. "Katie, I hope you know even though I haven't been a good husband or father for many years. I have always loved you. I have tried to respect your love for Raphael that I could always see in your eyes at the mention of his name. Thanks for taking care of me for so many years. You deserved better.

Katie squeezed his hand and kissed him on the cheek. "I love you, too, Keith. You have always been the best friend I've ever had in my life. We have laughed together, cried together, and fought battles together. You brought the kids lots of happiness and some heartaches but they both love you, especially Karley Bug."

Keith looked at her and smiled. "All those women, Katie, they didn't mean anything to me." "I know, Keith," Katie said. I wish I could have been a better wife to you.

The medication was wearing off and he was becoming restless. The nurse gave him another shot and he went to sleep. Later that night both kids came in to see him. He managed to talk to both of them alone. Katie went out to give them some time to say goodbye. She never asked what happened between them.

Katie never left the hospital. She would shower and change clothes in his bathroom.

As his pain increased, so did his medication. The left side of his head was cold while the right side sweated profusely. He never spoke a word after the day he talked to Katie and the kids until 11:15pm, July 18, he opened his eyes for the last time and said, "my Karley Bug." Karla and Katie were holding his hands when he passed away. He was 64 years old and he and Katie had been in their strange marriage for 46 years.

After the emotional funeral was over and Katie came home to the empty house, she finally cried for the first time. She cried because no one needed her. She cried because she thought she would be lonely. She was apprehensive about her future.

Karla and Matt came often for the first couple of weeks offering to help her with something or just visiting or to take her to dinner.

But, of course, they soon got back into their normal routine with their families.

Wasn't long until Katie went back to her own routine before Keith had gotten so ill, part-time job, gym, and babysitting with the grandkids.

She was a very attractive 75 year old with a figure younger women envied. Her silver hair would glow in the sunlight. She thought young and always had some kind of project she was working on.

A friend suggested her getting on a dating site on the internet. She thought it might be fun and tried it. She had two dates and decided it was not for her.

It was over a year since Keith had died when she decided to finally clean his stuff out of his bedroom and make a guest room there. She could really use that extra closet.

She started with the dresser. She found things she wanted to give the kids, things to give to charity and some junk for the dumpster.

At one corner of a drawer she found a small stack of letters. They had a woman's name with the return address. Katie looked at the postmark dates 2008-2009. That was the year before and the year he was ill. She opened one of the letters. It was definitely a love letter with strong sexual content. She took that letter and the rest without reading them to the garbage. They were Keith's private life and she didn't want to pry anymore.

You sexy little devil, she thought and smiled. Typical Keith, she reminded herself and kept working on her cleaning project.

The following weeks she shopped for new bed linens, bedspread, and drapes. Before she painted, she had Matt put in a new ceiling fan. She now had a pretty guest room but no guest she laughed.

She would like to have had Lisa come visit her but they had lost contact years ago. Matt was six the last time she saw her.

She thought of Raphael a lot and wondered if she would ever see him again. She had made herself busy through the years but he was always popping up in her mind. She knew she would always love him and still dreamed of being in his arms.

Liz came over often after Keith died to check on her and just to be company for her.

This morning, Emily called early. "Katie, I am dying for some of your chocolate chip pancakes, how about it, can you feed a hungry sister?" "Sure," Katie told her.

Katie hurried with her shower and pulled on a pair of jeans and a pretty yellow tee, grabbed a pair of yellow flip flops, slightly gelled her short grey hair and finished up with pink lip gloss.

She had just finished setting the table when Liz popped in the door. "Morning, Sis," she said. "Hi," Katie responded. "You sure are a pretty lady, Katie," Liz told her while she gave her a hug. "Thanks, you aren't so bad yourself," she told her sister.

They sat down and ate pancakes and nibbled on a bowl of strawberries and bananas and emptied the pot of coffee.

After they finished breakfast and talked for an hour it was near eleven o'clock. "May I use your phone, Katie? I need to call the contractor that is building our garage, he never finished the trim and it has been four weeks," Liz told her. "Sure," Katie answered, "Do you need the phone book?" "Yes, I guess so, I forgot his card," she said. His name is Jerry Wilford.

Liz was going down the names in the phonebook, suddenly she looked up at Katie. "Is this who I think it is, Katie?" "Don't know, who do you think it is?" Katie asked her. She went over to see the name she was pointing at, Raphael Willis.

Katie's stomach did a flip flop and she thought she was going to lose her breakfast. "Probably not," she squeaked. "Call and see Emily urged her. "No, I'm not calling," Katie said, "What if it is him, no, I won't do it." "Why not?" Liz said, "I know you still love him." "Don't be silly, Liz," Katie answered but knew she would someday. Emily was the only person who knew Matt was Raphael's son. "Well then, I am going to call and talk to him after all we grew up together." "Do what you want," Katie said, hoping she would and he would ask about her.

His phone rang several times but no one answered. "Don't leave a message, hang up," Katie told her.

In about ten minutes, Katie's phone rang. She answered it without looking at the caller ID. It was a female voice, "Did you call the Willis residence a few minutes ago?" she asked. Katie was caught off guard and didn't know what to say. She knew the woman had seen her name on her caller ID.

"Yes, I was looking for a friend of my brother's from years ago," she stuttered. His name was Raphael Willis, I saw it in the phonebook when I was looking for someone else."

"I know who you are, Katie, hold on a minute." Katie heard her yell, "Raphael, it's your old girlfriend, Katie."

Raphael picked up the phone. "Hello, this is Raphael, he said in the same sexy voice he always had that Katie could never forget. "Hi, Katie, How are you doing, haven't talked to you for thirty years or so." "Been far too long." "How's Keith and your family?" Raphael could always ask a dozen questions in five minutes.

Katie butt in, "Raphael, Keith died two years ago from cancer. Matt Jr. is doing fine. He has one daughter and three grandkids." "I'm a great grandmother and I love it." Katie stopped and let him talk again. "I don't have any kids except Matt and I have never heard from him," Raphael told her. "I thought he would look me up when he was 18 but he never did and I didn't even know what state you were living in."

"He doesn't know about you," Katie told him with tears in her eyes.

"I want to come see you, Katie, I think we need to talk, seriously. What are you doing tomorrow, can I come over?"

"Not tomorrow, Raphael," she laughed, "unless you are interested in some makeup as I am giving a makeup party at my house tomorrow. Of course, maybe your wife would like to come, what is her name, I seem to have forgotten," "sorry," Katie said in a casual manner.

"No, no one but me will be there party or not, what is your address?" he asked.

Katie gave him her address not knowing if he was serious about coming or not.

She said "Goodbye," and started laughing. "He says he is coming to my makeup party tomorrow," she told Liz. "That's the Raphael I know, always where the girls were," Liz said.

"I wonder if he looks anything like he used to," Liz commented. "Well, he told me he was bald and had a grey beard," Katie said.

Katie got so excited, she shouted, "yes, yes, yes" and jumped up and down. "I can't wait to see him," she told Liz. "I can't believe that he has been this close to me and I couldn't feel it."

CHAPTER 29

The next day Raphael showed up at the party just as he said he would.

Katie saw a green Sebring pull up in the driveway and park. Doesn't look like Raphael's taste in cars, she thought but then he is now an old man, that she couldn't picture! All the party guests had arrived around an hour ago. She ran out of the house.

She watched as this tall thin guy with a short white beard stepped from the car. He was still handsome. She ran to him and threw her arms around him. He hugged her for at least a minute before he spoke. "Katie, my goodness you look just like you did years ago. I would have known you had I seen you anywhere." Katie looked into his eyes, yep it was Raphael, those eyes never changed.

"Raphael, I'm so happy to see you," Katie finally found her voice. "Me too," he answered.

They went into the house and she introduced him as her friend to those who did not know him. Of course, her sisters knew who he was.

His granddaughter Karla was there but she didn't know who he was and wondered why her Grandmother had invited a man to a makeup party.

Liz was beside herself. She did not miss that Raphael's eyes almost never left Katie while she finished up the party.

Raphael talked with her sisters and commented on the beautiful children in the playroom. He also thought their mother was gorgeous and reminded him of his aunt. Liz brought the 8 month old baby and sat her on his lap.

"This is the sweetest thing I have ever seen," he said and remembered how a few years ago he wished he had raised Matt and had beautiful grandchildren like this. He really hoped that he would see his son even if he couldn't tell him who he was.

After everyone left, he told Katie he had to go, but he wanted to see her tomorrow, so they could talk.

Katie said yes that they had a lot to talk about. Katie told him that Karly was his granddaughter and the three lovely children were his great grandchildren.

"You mean to tell me that beautiful lady is my granddaughter and those precious children are my great grandbabies," Raphael almost cried. Big tears were about to escape from those big sad eyes. "But they don't know who I am," he said sadly.

"They will, Raphael, I'm telling Karly Wednesday when I see her. She will be shocked but she is open-minded and will accept you after she gives it some thought," Katie said.

"Now, Matt is a different story. I will have to ask him if he wants to meet you after I tell him the story. He probably won't accept you at first, but give him some time and I think he will later.

Raphael came back the next day as he had suggested. "Would you like to go to lunch with me, Katie?" "We can go to Lexington at this great restaurant where I go a lot and we can have some privacy, and the two hour ride will give us time to talk.

On the drive to Lexington, Katie tried to explain her 46 years with Keith, and him knowing that she loved Raphael for the duration of their marriage.

Raphael explained why he had married Sandy and how he had worked at having a home and to make the marriage work. Two weeks ago before my call to him they had decided on getting a divorce, he said. "It will get nasty," he advised her, there is quite a bit of money involved."

"We were arguing at the time you called," Raphael said. "That call was fuel for the fire." "She said that she knew I had been seeing you or you would not have called."

"We have not lived together as husband and wife for twenty years." "We are roommates and not happy ones at that." Raphael paused and Katie hugged him. "I have never stopped loving you," she told him. "I know you don't believe me, but I have missed you all these years, I guess you could say I loved you too, just couldn't label it with one word," he answered.

"I would like the kids to know who I am, especially my son," he told her. "We could all get together and explain the whole story to them and try to get to know each other and put an end to this sad story and start a happier one," he suggested. "If you can ever truly forgive me."

"Katie, maybe you could help me to enjoy my family. Maybe I don't deserve it, but I will try to make it up to them," he said frustrated.

"Think about it, Katie and if you think you can accomplish that, call me." "I won't see you anymore if I don't hear from you," he said. He gave her a hug and held her a little longer than a casual hug.

The next week Katie got up the nerve to tell the kids. She had not heard from Raphael. She tried to explain the situation to Matt and Karla the best she could alone.

Karla said she would always love Granddaddy but she would like to get to know Raphael better since he was her real genetic grandfather.

Matt said he had heard that name mentioned before and wondered who he was. "I have been without him for 48 years, and he never bothered to find me. I don't think I want to meet him at this late date," Matt made it clear he was not interested in him. "Why, Mom, would you keep a secret like that from me for so many years? I don't even want an answer," he said.

A week later, Matt stopped in to see her, "O.K. Mom, I think I want to meet this so called Dad of mine after all." "Won't promise what I will say but let's do it." "We will set up a date, I will let you know," Katie told him.

Kate was called and she and Matt agreed on Friday evening at a local restaurant.

Katie called Raphael, he answered the phone, "O.K. Grandpa," Katie informed him, "it is all set up for me, Karla, Matt, and you to get together Friday night if that is feasible for you." "Thanks, Katie, you are the same gracious lady I remember," he answered.

Of course, Friday proved to be awkward for everyone. Raphael was very cordial and understanding of some very hard questions, so everyone decided to give the new family a try.

Matt understandably wanted a paternity test.

The relationships were proving to be favorable. Karla started inviting Raphael to the children's activities and the kids grew close to him almost immediately. He proved to be a skilled Grandfather.

It was amazing how much Raphael and Matt had in common establishing how much genes count in how we are individuals. They both loved the old vintage automobiles, both were into motorcycles, both non-drinkers and hard working guys.

Christmas 2011 came and Raphael was very generous with his gift giving with all the kids. He gave Karla a laptop and Matt a motorcycle. It was his first new one and he was thrilled.

Raphael spent a lot of time with all the kids, but Katie saw him only at the kids activities. They spoke only about the children and he never hugged her again since that big long hug in August when he was leaving after their talk. She would sometimes catch him staring at her as he did when he was a child. If she looked back at him, he would stop staring and focus his attention on the children. She often wondered what he was thinking but would never ask.

After a rough winter, Spring of 2012 finally arrived, none too soon for anyone. It was a sunny warm Saturday in April. Katie was cleaning in her garage. She heard a motorcycle approaching and she was happy. Must be Matt stopping to see her. She always loved seeing him.

When the bike turned into the drive she could see it was two bikes, Matt and Raphael. "Want to use your bathroom," Matt announced loudly before he cut the motor. "Of course," Katie replied.

Raphael went into the house and Matt talked to his Mom for a few minutes. "I'm really getting to know Raphael," he said. "I really like him a lot." "Wish I had known him years ago."

Raphael was soon back outside and Matt went into the house. Raphael came over and looked at Katie as only Raphael could. "Katie, I haven't seen you or talked to you because I don't want you in the middle of this divorce, it was in the process before you came into the picture and I want it to stay that way but I am so tired of waiting, I want to get to know you again," he told her.

"She has contested everything, so I am positive the divorce will take at least a year."

"Oh," he changed the subject, remember when you rode with me on my first Harley?" he asked. Katie smiled, "That was fun, of course, I remember." "Would you like to ride with me again?" Raphael asked. "That would be the most fun I've had in years," Katie assured him. Matt came back out and they both got ready to leave. "I'll call you later," Raphael yelled at her over the sound of two bike motors.

Four o'clock the phone rang. Katie's heart was beating like a warrior's drum. "Hello, Raphael," she answered like she was out of breath. "You O.K.? Raphael asked. "Yes, rushing," Katie lied. "Can be on this phone for only a minute," he said quietly. "Can you spend the day with me tomorrow?" "Yes," Katie answered him. "I will pick you up at 11:00am if that is O.K." "Yes," Katie said and Raphael said bye and that ended the conversation. She hardly got a minutes sleep that night, she was so excited.

Ten o'clock the next morning found Katie pacing the floor in well fitting jeans and a yellow sweater topped off with a pretty daisy print silk scarf and strappy yellow sandals, her favorite kind of shoe for a lifetime, finished her outfit.

Right on the dot of eleven, he pulled into the drive. She met him at the door. This time he hugged and kissed her. Katie was breathless. She had longed for that kiss for so long.

"Katie, you look exactly as you did when you were 30. You are beautiful," and hugged her again. "Have you had breakfast yet?" "No, just coffee," Katie answered him.

"Let's start the day with a breakfast then," "Are you ready to go?" he asked. "Yes," she said nodding.

They went to a waffle restaurant and had waffles with fruit and bacon with lots of fresh coffee. "Next we have to go to a Harley store and get you a helmet if we are going to ride the bike together," he told her assuming that she meant it when she told him it would be fun. The Harley store was exciting for Katie as it was the first one she had been in. After trying on several helmets, one finally fit. "You are so tiny, Katie, you are like a little Barbie Doll," Raphael said.

After they left the store, they rode around looking at places that reminded them of their youth, they found the apartment where Katie lived the first time Raphael made love to her and went to Deer Horn Lake. At 4:30 they were starved, so they stopped and had an early dinner and he took her home.

The rest of the summer was spent on the bike. They went on short trips and sometimes long trips. They began to make new memories for the two of them.

Biking was the entirety of their summer together besides the times they went to see the great grandbabies or have dinner with Matt or Karla.

They had favorite scenic roads to enjoy and favorite towns and quaint little restaurants that were their favorite places to eat lunch. Sometimes Katie would pack a picnic lunch that Raphael would store in the saddle bags and they would ride to their favorite spot on the river or to Deer Horn Lake.

They both loved the restaurant located on a cliff overlooking the Ohio River.

Raphael would always hug her when he came to pick her up and kiss her bye when he left but he never touched her intimately or kissed her sexually. She thought he wanted to be a good friend and she loved him enough to give him what he wanted but at night, she would think of him making love to her again. She thought maybe because she had gotten older that maybe he just wasn't attracted to her anymore.

The weather had changed and it was too cold for biking. It was almost Thanksgiving. Katie had not heard from Raphael for three weeks. Karla said she had seen the kids, but he never picked Katie up to go with him, but she knew she would see him again. Out of the blue, one afternoon Raphael called and asked if she was alone. "Yes," Katie said and asked "Why?". "I want to see you right now Katie, it can't wait," Raphael said and sounded anxious. She just knew he was going to tell her that he couldn't see her anymore. She thought that he might be telling her a lie about getting a divorce or they were calling it off. She was almost in tears. I can't live without him again she told God as she tried to calm down and tell Raphael to come on over.

Within the hour, Raphael walked through the door without knocking or ringing the door bell. She gave him a small worried grin.

Before she could say hello, Raphael grabbed her and pulled her to him and gave her a long sexy kiss. Katie threw her arms around his neck and they pressed their bodies together as close as they could get. Katie felt him wanting her. She was drowning in sensations she once thought were gone forever. She knew it was time. She couldn't talk, she took his hand and quietly led him to her bedroom. He followed her willingly.

Raphael kissed her again, asking for her love in actions, not words. Katie unbuttoned his shirt, he had taken off his jacket and thrown it on the couch before they went to the bedroom.

His chest was covered with silky white hair. She got a scent of a manly soap, he must have gotten out of the shower a short time ago, she thought.

Raphael pulled her tee over her head revealing a bra full of the same small firm breasts from decades ago. He turned her around to unfasten her bra and noticed her little round fannie that still filled out her jeans.

How could a 78 year old woman look like this, "You are still beautiful my Katie," Raphael told her as he picked her up and laid her on the bed. He then reached down and pulled off her jeans, but left on her adorable yellow lace panties.

Raphael then slipped his own jeans off and laid them across a chair.

Katie was thinking as she watched him, his manhood pushing against his underwear, it was the same scene as she remembered over fifty years ago. Raphael took off his underwear releasing it from its bounds. It now stood straight and proud.

He showed Katie he was still desirable and sexy at 68.

Raphael climbed in bed and lay beside Katie. She ran her hand from his thigh to his erection. He began touching her and kissing her all over.

He reached down and slowly pulled her panties off her butt and down her legs.

He pitched them on the floor beside the bed.

He kissed her throat, between her breasts, his tongue running down her tummy to her belly button. He followed from her belly button to her mound of shining silver hair. His tongue quickly found her clitoris. He made love to her with only his mouth for a full five minutes. Katie had never experienced anything like it, not even with him.

She was going crazy. Right before she was ready to climax, he stopped and laid down beside her again.

"Are you o.k. for sex, Katie?" he asked concerned only for her. "I think so Raphael, it has been a lot of years," she answered truthfully.

"We will go slowly," he said entering her carefully. It slipped in easy and it wasn't long before he forgot the easy.

Katie wrapped her legs around his back and stars were twinkling all around her. They both lost reality in all the ecstasy and suddenly it was over.

"Katie, I have missed you so much," Raphael told her as he held her in his arms. "I have missed you all my life," she told him and kissed him on that sexy mouth she always adored.

"Katie, I have something to tell you," Raphael said. Katie shuddered thinking he was leaving again. He looked her in the eyes with that serious look he was so good at.

"Katie, my love, I am a free man." "I have been wanting to make love to you since the first day I saw you in August but I decided to wait until the day I could deliver this wonderful news.

Katie hugged him so tightly he had to cough to get his breath.

CHAPTER 30

Christmas 2013 brought happiness to everyone. Both Karla's and Matt's families and, of course, Raphael came to Katie's for Christmas dinner.

"The kids kept asking when they could open their gifts. You have to help me get dinner first," Katie told them.

Matt and his wife had brought baked sweet potatoes, spinach salad, and apple pies.

Karla and her husband had made Karla's famous green bean casserole, corn with sweet red peppers, and homemade bread.

Raphael had brought the turkey and helped Katie prepare it with dressing and his favorite mashed potatoes with turkey gravy and buttered baby peas. And, of course, Katie had to make the kids beloved mac and cheese.

What a dinner. Everyone had eaten so much and with the help of the turkey evceryone was ready for a nap. The little ones wanted none of that however. The minute the last crumb was cleaned up they ran to Katie announcing it was time to open gifts.

The kids gave Katie new framed pictures of themselves and a box of her sinful dark chocolate.

Of course, the kids had gotten their most coveted toys. The adults received gift certificates from their favorite restaurants and specialty stores.

Katie gave Raphael an old picture of her from 1964 in a leather frame and a gift certificate from his man toy store, The Harley Davidson Store. Matt was envious. Good thing Raphael had gotten him one.

After all the other gifts were opened, Raphael took a small wrapped box from his pocket and handed it to Katie. "Merry Christmas, Katie," he said.

She opened the box to find a small tasteful silver Harley logo ring, the inside of the logo was filled with diamonds. "This is to remember our wonderful past summer," Raphael said, "and I intend for us to have many, many more." He kissed her lightly on the top of her head and squeezed her hand as he put the ring on the ring finger of her right hand.

Katie thanked him and said she loved it but did not need anything to remind her of the most fun summer of her life.

Karla teased her, "Mom is that an engagement ring?" "Not Harley," she said and laughed, "I mean not hardly."

After all, the kids went home, Raphael said he had had a wonderful day but the night should be even better. He had planned on spending the night with her. They went to bed and he made love to her for a good hour. She fell asleep in his arms, exhausted.

The following morning, they got up late, had cereal for breakfast, both were still full from Christmas dinner.

After cleaning up from yesterday, they sat down to rest. Raphael put his arm around her and said he had a question for her. "Katie, if I take over all the expenses and do some remodeling in your house, could I move in with you?" "I would be with you more and could be a tremendous help financially."

"I will think about it," Katie said. She wanted that so badly, but had to see what the kids would think about the situation.

The kids thought it was a great idea. They hated their Mom being alone since Keith died and they both admired Raphael how he jumped right into being family from the beginning.

Raphael moved in right away and the next year was a busy one. Raphael kept his word and helped Katie with some extensive remodeling. The house looked great inside and out.

Katie loved cooking for Raphael and being with him every day was a life-long dream come true.

On Valentine's Day, Raphael gave Katie a big red satin covered heart Valentine card. When she opened the heart, it had one big hand written message inside, "Katie, will you marry me?"

Katie couldn't believe this was happening. She put her arms around him and looked into those eyes she had remembered for a lifetime.

"Yes, Raphael, that was a dream she would never have allowed herself to dream. Of course, I will marry you," she finally finished. Katie went to the kitchen to make lunch. "Katie, Raphael was yelling for her from the living room. Katie went into the living room, "Sit by me for a moment, Katie, I have a request of you," Raphael said. Raphael looked serious, "Yes, what is it?" Katie asked.

"Katie," Raphael began, "I hope you won't plan on a pricey traditional wedding." "I am a simple man and swore I would never put on another tie after retiring." "I would like for it to be small and simple. I will be happy if we can be married in the back yard or here in the living room," he said. "And the fewer people, the better," he finished."

"Do you have any suggestions?" he asked.

"Let me think about it, Raphael, this was a surprise to me," she anwered. "Did you have a date in mind?" she asked.

"I hope you will be happy with simple but still feel like I have been married, my last two were nothing, and neither were the marriages," Katie told him not waiting for him to answer about the date.

"This time if I get married, I want a real minister of a church to marry me." Is that O.K. with you, Raphael?"

"Go ahead and make your plans," he said. "We will then go over them together and if there is something I can't live with, I will let you know."

"Once again, I will remind you "Simple", that's me, we have lived together for a year now, so you should know that," he said and grinned.

Katie suggested the first Saturday in June for the wedding. "Should be nice weather if we want it outside and that will give us almost four months to plan," she told him.

"That's ok," he said and got up to go to the kitchen, "Let's have lunch." After lunch, they sat at the table and Katie began to make plans again.

Raphael insisted that he would wear jeans and Katie thought maybe a cute sundress with her favorite, her strappy sandals would be appropriate for an outside wedding in June.

"I would like flowers, a few decorations, and a photographer," Katie added. "You are soon going to have a traditional wedding planned, Katie, "Simple," he once again stated.

May the 1st came and no definite plans were made. "We must sit down and finalize the wedding plans today," Katie told him after breakfast.

"No, we don't, Katie, can we just elope or leave things the way it is, I am happy, are you?" he asked and went out to the garage.

Karla came in and overheard Raphael's frustration. She motioned Katie to follow her to the garage. "You guys are getting nowhere. Why don't you forget about it and let me plan everything except the location?" "I promise you I will take care of the rest and it will be fun and simple.

"Of course, Matt and I will want to be your only attendants," she said.

Raphael and Katie agreed that would be a great idea. "See," Raphael said, "the best man and maid of honor was chosen that quickly.

"Katie, how about us going to get rings today and that will be one more task completed," Raphael said, just wanting to get it all done.

Three hours later they came home with a white gold band for Raphael and a white gold band with a circle of diamonds around the entire ring for Katie.

The next day, Raphael asked Karla if she and the kids would like to join he and Katie for lunch. They were going to drive to the Overlook Restaurant overlooking the Ohio River. It was one of Raphael's bike rides about 30 miles from their home, but today they were driving and he loved having the grandkids for a few hours.

It was a nice sunny day in the upper 70's and they all wanted to eat on the outside patio and watch the boats go down the river. The kids loved it.

As they were eating lunch, Raphael pointed out a beautiful weeping willow tree down the hill closer to the river. "That's where I would like to have the wedding, girls," he said to Karla and Katie. Perfect they all said almost in unison. Raphael was surprised when he realized one more detail of the wedding was checked off the list.

One afternoon the next week, Raphael came home from his monthly East Professional Bikers Club meeting and announced to Katie that his friend, Dennis, the Club Chaplain and pastor of the Saints Christian Church agreed to marry them at the Overlook on June 6th. Raphael said he told him he was wanting a reason to ride his bike up there anyway. Raphael told him that he and Katie would probably ride his bike too, the wedding was going to be very informal.

He then gave Katie that cute Raphael smile and asked if she approved.

Within the next few days, Karla called Katie and told her the wedding plans were complete. "Thank God," Katie said, "I don't care about anything anymore except that I want to marry Raphael and by a minister.

CHAPTER 31

June 6, 2015. The day had arrived that Katie had waited for all her life.

The sun was warm, but not too hot. The sky was blue with only a few white fluffy clouds moving slowly across the sky like white sail boats moving in the gentle breeze blowing off the river. A perfect day for an outside wedding.

Under the big willow tree Matt and Karla had placed a huge metal heart wrapped in turquoise satin ribbon with clumps of real pink rose buds attached to the top of the heart.

Just like Matt, Raphael was wearing a turquoise tee with his jeans and Karla a pink tee with her jeans and Katie a pink tee matching Karla's except hers had the words "Raphael Forever" written on the back in turquoise bling.

Dennis did indeed ride his bike as did Raphael and Katie.

Everyone took their places under the tree, Raphael and Katie framed by the heart.

Dennis had promised he would keep the ceremony short but perfect.

Close to 100 bikers watched from atop the parking lot at the restaurant. Dennis had announced the wedding date to as many of the biker club members that he could reach. Some came with their wives or girlfriends and some rode alone.

Dennis read the scripture from the Bible, prayed, and then asked Raphael if he wished to say his own vows. "Yes," Raphael said and took Katie's hands.

"Katie, I will hold you in my heart and in my arms for as long as we both shall live."

"I will protect you from physical and emotional harm forever to the best of my abilities."

"I will always be your best friend, your protector, and lover for the rest of my life. Katie, will you accept me as your husband?" "Yes," Katie answered and Raphael placed the ring on her ring finger, this time on her left hand.

Now, it was Katie's turn. She took Raphael's hands and looked into those brown eyes she had loved forever. She saw so much love reflected in those eyes she wanted to cry with joy.

"Raphael," Katie began, "I will always be beside you through bad times and good times, through sickness and health."

"Whether we are rich or poor in material possessions, I will always be rich in your love."

"I will always respect your simple way of life and the love you have for God's world and all the creatures in it."

"I will appreciate your passions for bike riding, sailing, fishing, and gun collecting and we will enjoy the out-of-doors together."

"Raphael, today I surrender to you my heart, body, and soul, and you will truly be my Raphael forever."

"Raphael, will you take me for your wife?"

"Yes, my sweet Katie," Raphael answered while Katie placed the wedding band on his finger.

Dennis then pronounced them husband and wife. Raphael happily kissed his bride.

Karla had strayed somewhat from Raphael's idea of simple. She had hired a photographer for the wedding. She thought her grandmother deserved that. Her favorite picture was of Katie and Raphael standing inside the heart. she knew that would be Katie's favorite also.

A luncheon was held for the couple inside the Overlook Restaurant. When Dennis told a few of the club members about the wedding, the message was soon passed on to other members. The club members gave the luncheon as a wedding gift to the couple. The restaurant baker had baked them a three tier cake with a motorcycle on top and "May you always be happy" written around the bottom layer. It was trimmed in turquoise and pink rose buds.

Soon the restaurant had to open up to the general public and everyone left except the bride and groom.

They wanted to walk back down to the willow tree and think about what had just happened. the heart was gone, but it was a beautiful place on the river bank to lull around and watch the activity on the river.

After a short bike ride, they came back to the restaurant for dinner and sat outside on the patio to watch the sunset on the river.

The ride back home was like a fairy tale with a million tiny stars sparkling over head. Even the bike sounded peaceful. Katie had never been on the bike at night. The stretch of road with woods on both sides was like passing through another world. The only lights were the stars and the bike light guiding them through the darkness. Once in a while the moon would break through an opening in the trees.

When they arrived home, they showered, put on their robes and had a glass of wine and then off to the bedroom.

It had been a long amazing day. It was all so surreal to Katie that a fifty year dream could finally come true.

The thrills began when Raphael held her close to his marvelous body and his natural manly aroma took over her senses.

His desirable lips were like a magnet drawing her lips to his. They were like a liquid satin covering her mouth., his tongue sweet and searching. His kisses filled her whole being with desire, running the length of her body, now begging for more.

Raphael removed his robe and threw it over a chair his naked body only exciting her more. She loved the grey curls covering his chest and yearned to be brushed against them.

His beast-like prowess was standing out straight and hard boasting of his manhood.

He reached down and pulled Katie's robe from her shoulders and let it drop to the floor while still kissing her. He gently picked her up and laid her on the bed and got in beside her.

His magic hands took over and Katie began to shake in anticipation.

Lightning flashed throughout her body as he filled her with that exciting mystery.

The thrills were indescribable and Katie kept telling him, "I love you, Raphael," over and over.

Raphael then took her tenderly in his arms and whispered, "I love you, too, Mrs. Willis."

Katie's heart and body were now deliriously happy and she knew as always that it would be Raphael forever.

CHAPTER 32

Ten years went by quickly and Katie and Raphael were beginning to age but their love for each other deepened as time went by.

Raphael has developed congestive heart failure and decided to give up biking. He had given his bike to Matt so that he and Katie would see it occasionally when Matt rode it to see them when he could.

Katie was now in her 80's but Raphael said she was still beautiful.

The grand kids were getting older but was still close and were very protective of their beloved grand parents.

It was early Saturday morning, the sun was shining brightly around the curtains. Katie woke suddenly and wondered why she has jumped out of bed so quickly. She always woke up in Raphael's arms and they would lie there and talk for a while before getting up and making coffee.

She glanced over at the bed where she had exited so quickly. Raphael was not there. "Raphael" she yelled thinking he was across the room in the bath. Her heart was pounding, "Why am I panicking" she said aloud.

She glanced in the bath room, but Raphael was not there. She ran down the hallway and heard him in the other bath room groaning. She saw him bent over the sink throwing up. He looked pale and like he was in pain. "Raphael Sweetheart" she said as she went to him, "Whatever is the matter?" He could not answer her. She helped him back to bed and grabbed the phone to call 911. He had grabbed his chest in pain. Katie feared he was having a heart attack. She explained to the operator that her husband was having severe chest pain and she needed an ambulance right away. She was shaking as she gave the lady her address.

"I think it is getting better" Raphael whispered. "I think I would like a cup of coffee." "No Raphael, you are going straight to the hospital" Katie said, tears escaping from her eyes and rolling down her cheeks. She picked up Raphael's hand and it felt so cold. "It is going to the O.K she thought and believed it, after all he was Raphael and she needed him.

Six minutes later the ambulance arrived. While the M.T.S' were putting Raphael in the ambulance, Katie grabbed her purse and keys. She had managed to slip into a pair of jeans and shirt and her shoes the few minutes it took the ambulance to arrive.

She ran to the ambulance and kissed Raphael's forehead. He opened his eyes and have her a weak little smile.

As she followed the ambulance to the hospital, she prayed, "Please God don't take Raphael yet." She thanked God for bringing him back to her and for giving her all these wonderful years with him.

Katie parked the car and ran to meet Raphael going through the door to the emergency room. She noticed he had grown paler and it was difficult for him to talk or even breathe.

Staff told her they would get the paper work done later. They put a name tag on his wrist and headed to I.C.U. With him. He was still on the ambulance stretchers and two doctors were working on him enroute.

Raphael turned his head and looked at her, "I have always loved your Katie", he managed to whisper. Raphael then took one deep breath and died before reaching I.C.U.

Katie felt herself falling. When she became conscious, she was in the emergency room on a stretcher, one nurse taking her blood pressure and one holding her hand. One of them and that she has fainted and that Raphael has died as she already knew.

She knew she had to stay strong for the kids as she had always.

Katie called both Matt and Karla explaining the situation. They both told her they would be there as soon as possible.

They both arrived at the same time. Karla ran over and put her arms around her grandmother and started to cry. "What can I do?" she asked Katie. "It's just like Granddaddy died again" Karla said.

Matt came over where she was sitting and put his arms around her but said nothing, just started at her with the same expression that was just like Raphael.

The next few days were busy making arrangements for the funeral and all the other necessities. Katie was strong as every one expected her to be, but her heart was so broken she wasn't sure she would ever feel again.

Raphael had left her all the money she would ever need and took care of the children as he had intended.

The days went by, weeks, months, even a couple of years. Katie was never the same person. She dis things with Matt, Karla and the grand kids. Sometimes she smiled and even laughed when it was appreciate and expected to do so. But she had lost her eternal youthfulness and her glow was gone.

Karla began to worry about her grandmother. Katie was not the same Katie she was a year ago, she had walked almost daily all her life, but now never wanted to go outside. She was always happy to see the kids stop by but seldom went to Karla's and never to Matt's fearing that he would have the garage door open and she would see Raphael's bike. Matt never rode his biked to his mom's house any more.

Katie ate very little and now weighed 97 lbs. Her doctor was worried about her and talked to Karla about maybe seeing her grandmother more often encouraging her to go out to lunch or dinner more often.

Karla tried to talk with Katie, "Grandmother" Karla began, "Where is all that spark and energy, that lust for life you always had?" "Raphael would be disappointed in you," she continued.

"Mind your own business, I am 86 and entitled to live the way I want," Katie snapped back at her. "You never wanted to take care of your own affairs when we were in school together" she added.

Karla was shocked and really looked at Katie for the first time in a long time Katie was staring at the wall, no expression in her eyes what so ever. "Who are you talking to Grandmother, do you know who I am?" Katie looked at Karla and seemed to recognize her. "Of course I know who you are Karla, I guess you now think I am crazy", Katie said and laughed out loud. Karla laughed with her and thought she must have been thinking of something from her school days.

A couple of days went by and Katie had not called Karla. She was alarmed because Katie called her every day even if Karla had gone to see her that day. So she called Katie but there was no answer. Karla was scared. She ran straight to her car and drove to Katie's, a half hour away. She parked the car and ran to the house. The door was open and she went in calling, "Grandmother where are you?"

Katie was sitting on the couch wrapped in a blanket that belonged to Raphael, he likes in the winter to wrap up and watch T.V., but it was the first of September and warm.

"Hi" Karla said, "Why didn't you call e or answer me when I called you?" Karla questioned Katie "Just sitting here talking to Raphael," replied Katie and patted the pillow beside her. Karla tried to explain to Katie that no one was there but her. Katie became really irate and looked like she was going to hit Karla.

Karla went to the kitchen to see if there was signs that Katie had been eating. She found a skillet on the stove with burned eggs, shells and all but the stove had been turned off I have to get her to the doctor Karla said to herself.

"Grandmother, do you know who I am?" Karla ask once again. "Of course I know who you are Karla," Katie answered. "Well we almost forgot your doctor's appointment today, but if we hurry we can make it", Karla told her. Of course Katie did not have an appointment today but Karla was going to see if she would see her anyway.

"I am going to the bath room while you find you a sweater, it may be a bit cool for you since I found you all cuddled up in that blanket", she told her grandmother.

But while Katie was finding a sweater Karla went to the bath room and called Dr. Maupin and told her how strange Katie was acting and about skilled full of eggs and egg shells. Dr. Maupin told her to bring Katie right in that she could have had a stroke.

After examining Katie Dr. Maupin told her to wait for her, she would be right back, but she motioned Karla out in the hallway with her. "I think we need to put Katie in the hospital for a few test", she informed Karla. "She has no signs of having a stroke but is undernourished and dehydrated."

After 2 days of running test and giving her I.V's to hydrate her, Doctor Maupin told Karla was in the first stages of Alzheimer's and could no longer live alone.

Karla made arrangements for Katie to come to her home while she and her husband took care of all the legal issues involved.

After a month of taking care of Katie, Karla knew she would soon have to make permanent living arrangements for Katie as she needed to be wife and mother again.

With help from Dr. Maupin and other health experts, a really nice and efficient nursing facility was found.

Katie didn't seem to mind, just ask if she and Raphael were moving to a new house and told Karla there was nothing wrong with their old house.

After getting Katie settled in with what she needed at the nursing home, Karla set Katie's wedding pictures on her dresser and kissed her goodbye. "See you tomorrow" Karla said. Katie looked alarmed and told Karla she had forgotten Raphael's clothes. Karla hugged her again and told her she would bring them tomorrow.

While cleaning out Katie's house getting it ready to put on the market, Karla found a men's tee shirt yellowed with age but folded nicely in the bottom of a drawer. It must be at least 60 years old, Karla thought. She carefully picked it up to prevent it from falling apart, under it she found a picture of Raphael at the age of 19 or

20 she assumed, or maybe younger. She carefully put them in a bag without unfolding the shirt. She would take them to Katie tomorrow.

The next day, Karla took the shirt and picture to Katie. She seemed to be confused but hugged them up to her body and smiled which she seldom did any more.

The following day when Karla went to check on her, Katie was completely different person. She was mean and nasty to Karla. "Why are you messing with my stuff?" Katie screamed at her "and how did you get in my house?" Where is Raphael, she continued "Why did you run him away?" Katie began to cry and looked at Karla with a confused look and Karla thought she was going to hit her.

Karla called a nurse in who suggested that she give Katie her medication and that Karla should go home and let Katie nap and settle down. "She will be different when she wakes up", the nurse told her. Karla left the nursing home hurt and crying. She loved her grandmother so much but could not deal with her combative attitude toward her. She knew Katie did not recognize her but it still hurt.

The next day was a beautiful day and she asked Matt if he would ho with her. "I can't face her alone today", Karla told him. Matt seldom went to visit his mother any more. He had a hard time accepting her thinking he was Raphael or just not recognizing him at all.

Karla and Matt walked into Katie's room after taking a big breath before entering. Katie turned her head and looked at them. She smiled and held her arms out to hug Matt. "It's Matt, hi Karla Baby." I am so happy you could come visit me, I should be leaving the hospital soon, I can't wait to get back home, Raphael and I could go bike riding with you Matt if I wasn't sick." "What's wrong with me, I feel fine."

Karla hugged her grandmother and said. "I love you so much grandmother." "How are the kids?" Katie asked. "Oh they are O.K and I will soon be a grandmother also, Lindy's baby is due in two weeks." Karla told her. Katie did not respond and looked confused.

Karla asked Katie if she wanted anything to eat or drink. "The nurse is bringing me an orange juice in a minute," Katie told her.

"I'll go get it, you visit with Matt" Karla told her, wanting to talk to a nurse about how Katie had changed overnight. The nurse explained that it was unknown how or why these patients sometimes have brief periods of remembering a bit of their prior lives and people before the disease set in, but one thing for sure it would not last long.

Karla took Katie's juice to her and Katie hugged her. "This is a nice hospital, every body has been so kind to me since you brought me yesterday but I feel good now and am ready to go back home and Raphael," Katie told her. "Where is Raphael, he hasn't been here to see me today."

She quickly changed the subject and had that beautiful smile that Karla remembered since she was a child. Katie's eyes smiled when she smiled. Karla looked at her grandmother and could still see the beautiful lady she once was. Karla and Matt enjoyed visiting with Katie and stayed until Katie feel asleep. Karla left with Matt but planned to go back later while Katie knew who she was.

When Karla returned about four that afternoon Katie was sitting in her lounge chair. Someone had done her hair. Karla thought it was like silver thread woven into big loose curls. Karla also noticed she had put on her lip gloss, the only cosmetic she had brought with her.

Her face was glowing and her eyes sparkling. She looked at Karla and asked, "Is Raphael on his way, I am going home today.?" Karla was sad, she knew she had gotten back too late, but she also noticed that Katie seemed happy and not irritable as she normally was since she had become ill.

Karla sat on the side of Katie's bed since her room only had one chair and she was in it.

Katie was glowing when she asked Karla to help her back in her bed. Karla helped her back to bed and pulled her sheet up over her.

Katie turned her head toward the door as to look who was entering. "Raphael, my Raphael, you finally got here, I hope you rode the bike." "I'm ready Raphael" she said loudly and pulled her hand from Karla's.

At that time Katie sighed and closed her eyes but still had a smile on her face.

Somehow Karla knew she had died. Karla was surprised that she was not as upset as she thought that she would be. Karla was thankful that her Grandmother had known her and Matt that morning and had told them that she loved them.

Karla knew that Katie was finally where she wanted to be with Raphael.

Karla felt peace and even smiled a little smile as she left to get a nurse. She muttered very quietly, "yes it is truly Raphael forever this time."